Writers

T0153988

Writers

Antoine Volodine

Translated by Katina Rogers

DALKEY ARCHIVE PRESS
Champaign / London / Dublin

Originally published in French as *Écrivains* by Seuil, Paris, 2010

Copyright © 2010 by Seuil

Translation copyright © 2014 by Katina Rogers

First edition, 2014

Library of Congress Cataloging-in-Publication Data

Volodine, Antoine
    [Écrivains. English]
    Writers / Antoine Volodine; Translated by Katina Rogers. -- First Edition.

    pages cm
    "Originally published in French as Ecrivains by Seuil, Paris, 2010."
    ISBN 978-1-62897-040-1 (pbk. : alk. paper)
    I. Rogers, Katina L., translator. II. Title.
    PQ2682.O436E2713 2014
    843'.914--dc23

2014003173

Partially supported by the Illinois Arts Council, a state agency, and the University of Illinois (Urbana-Champaign).

The publication of this work was supported by a grant from the Centre national du livre (CNL)

www.dalkeyarchive.com

Cover: design and composition by Mikhail Iliatov;
Printed on permanent/durable acid-free paper

CONTENTS

EVERY NIGHT AT the bitterest hour, writer Mathias Olbane would get out of bed, where he had dozed fitfully since nightfall, assaulted by dreams and by hopelessness; without turning on the lights, he would go and sit in front of the bedroom mirror. The summer was interminable, the heat around him suffocating. The furniture and the floorboards creaked in the silence from time to time. The dust smelled of medicine, dried grass, hospital laundry. Mathias Olbane opened the dresser drawer under the mirror and unfolded the undershirt where he kept his pistol hidden; then, after making sure that the cartridge was in place, he closed the drawer, took off the safety, and pressed the weapon into his cheek, pointing the barrel towards the interior of his skull. Then he started to count. One ... two ... three ... four ... He counted slowly, without speaking aloud, but still forming the words with his lips. His mouth moved, and just below his jaw, at the spot where the tip of the pistol was lodged, his skin tightened and relaxed.

No lamps shone outside in the field that separated the house from the woods, but because he didn't close the bedroom's shutters when evening came, it wasn't pitch dark, and sometimes enough light filtered in from the countryside that he could catch his own gaze. It was a gaze without much intensity, and generally he responded with indifference, but once in a while he had the impression that he was face-to-face with an intruder who was watching him attempt to hide his emotions, and between his reflection and himself a kind of confrontation emerged. That disturbed him and sometimes caused him to muddle up his counting, and when he could no longer be certain exactly where he left off, he started again at zero, forbidding himself from then on to raise his eyes again to his own image.

Mathias Olbane's plan was to successfully kill himself before pronouncing the number four hundred and forty-four, which he had determined as the endpoint to this long mental ascent. Figuring one number every two seconds, the duration of his survival facing the mirror amounted to about fifteen minutes, which seemed reasonable to him. Moreover, four and forty-four referred to April 1944, the date of his paternal grandfather's death at Buchenwald. Numerology had never intrigued him and he didn't place mathematicians on any particular pedestal, but he did like the perfection that emanated from what he called beautiful numbers, and he also liked the idea of combining his desire for suicide with an homage to the disappeared, to one of the tragically disappeared members of his family.

The little convalescent home that his sister had chosen for him was located far from any major city, in the middle of the woods. He had no health insurance, and the fact that he had to count on the charity of his sister, who was in no easy financial situation herself, was for him additional grounds for melancholy. The window, slightly ajar, let in the murmur of poplars and birches when a breath of wind rustled through them, and until one in the morning, the hooting of tawny owls. Other sounds were rare. The nursing staff was off-duty until breakfast time. During the night, both nurses and patients slept. The bedrooms were well insulated, and if someone snored, groaned, or coughed, nobody heard it. Inside the building, as in its surroundings and secondary structures, the stillness of a cemetery reigned.

Before being admitted here, Mathias Olbane had spent more than a quarter-century in a high-security penitentiary for having committed several crimes in his day. We won't rehash his trial here. He had assassinated assassins, which is something that the law punishes, something that you pay for with a life sentence. He had served his time, and at fifty-three years old, while he was getting ready for a life of anonymity and discretion outside of the walls, he was afflicted with the illness. It was a terrible degenerative genetic disorder that had erupted suddenly, with no warning signs. With lightning speed, the illness had left his face unpleasant to look at, even monstrous. His skin cracked, a bloody dew pearled at the lips of his wounds, and in some places stains like cardboard appeared and spread, transforming his physiognomy into a geographic map of the world where imaginary continents promised degradation, lignification, and death to their citizens. Doctors agreed about the extreme rarity of the disease, and about its horrific symptoms and its incurable nature, but the name changed depending on the specialist. Mathias Olbane had adopted one at random and didn't mention it again unless he was truly obliged to speak about his case, such as in his nightmares, or when a new nurse's aide inquired about the results of his analyses or treatments. In those moments he said he suffered from an autoimmune oncoglyphosis. But the term disgusted him, and making the effort to pronounce it out loud plunged him into a state akin to shame.

One of the nocturnal symptoms of the oncoglyphosis was a retraction of the scalp. While Mathias Olbane, confronted by his dark image, slowly shelled out the numbers that were meant to be his last murmurs, the skin of his skull would clench, the pores would close up and, in some places, pull in the hairs by the root, as though inhaling them into his head. This swallowing-up didn't lead to the disappearance of his hair, but in the silence, it created a crackling sound, an inhuman sound that evoked the movements of insects and made you want to vomit. It was on hearing this sound that Mathias Olbane felt most acutely that it was time to be done with it. He started to pull the weapon's trigger. In an instant, his body was bathed in an icy sweat. Now's the time, he thought. Now or never.

And yet, while he seemed to have reached the decisive moment, he never took advantage of it to relive an accelerated flashback of his existence. His memory got stuck on two or three events whose insignificance he could not even measure, as though after his memory, he himself was struck by a violent intellectual paralysis, by an inability to make the distinction between the essential and the trivial. Quite often, the memories that presented themselves seemed to have surged up following a clumsy random selection. Accordingly, he once again saw a fight with a fellow inmate regarding poorly cleaned toilets, and then a walk he had taken along the edge of the forest, during which he had seen a grass snake. The snake slithered through a minuscule trickle of water and disappeared. These images repeated themselves, without changing, and then he came back to the bedroom, to the pistol, to the waiting. Crushed by the banality of the scenes that his mind regurgitated, drenched in a damp blend of sweat and lymph, he realized that he had interrupted his litany of numbers and that he had missed his chance to finally give the trigger one good pull.

He set the pistol down before him on the wooden tray with slightly tacky varnish and wiped his dripping hands on his pajama pants. Once again he palmed the weapon and pressed it against his cheek, and with tenacity but no buoyancy, he started his enumeration back at zero.

Before his arrest, Mathias Olbane had not been a prolific writer. Although obsessed by the need to write, he didn't feel the need to fashion pieces of prose with the goal of seeing them appear in a published work. He thought that the poetic game, the ephemeral assembly of words, the plunge into images, was an important dimension of his existence; but this activity, as urgent as it may have been, didn't deserve to wind up in a standardized volume, closed and dead on a bookshelf. He let his manuscripts lie dormant, didn't bother to finish them, and even theorized a bit on incompleteness, at least when his friends asked him how his creations were coming along. He spent several years like this without producing anything publishable, and then his pretense of belonging to the proud caste of unknown poets grew dull; his vision of himself as a creator vanished. Despite these circumstances, which were so inauspicious to literary emergence, and while he was devoting himself above all to underground battle and preparing for terrorist retaliation, in other words plotting many assassinations of assassins, and while everyone, himself included, thought that he had stopped writing, one day he gave a collection of stories to a sympathetic publisher, and the publisher made a small book out of them. The work was called *An Autumn at the Boyols*; it had a print run of a thousand copies and sold just under forty.

It consisted of eight short texts, inspired by fantasy or the bizarre, composed in a lusterless but impeccable style. Let's say that it was a collection that maintained a certain kinship with post-exoticism, and that, in that particular universe, could have passed as a collection of *entrevoûtes*. Mathias Olbane hadn't bent to any ideological constraint, except to not depicting conventional revolutionaries, or more generally, characters with stereotypical magical surrealist behavior. The only sympathetic critic, one who could have given a reaction in the press and had some authority with regard to the discovery of new talent, was baffled and didn't even mention the release of the book. In short, the failure of the publication was catastrophic. Nonetheless, two years later, Mathias Olbane, who had put the finishing touches to a second book, entrusted it to the same publisher. The latter, not at all discouraged by the desolate fate of *An Autumn at the Boyols'*, agreed to publish *Splendor of the Skiff*. It was a more ambitious novel from a literary point of view, in that it was a skillfully crafted work of fiction that simultaneously recounted a police investigation, several episodes of a global revolution, and traumatizing incursions into dream worlds. *Splendor of the Skiff* had a print run of five hundred copies. Its sales were markedly worse than the first book.

Thus ended the public career of Mathias Olbane as a man of letters.

During his trial, in which he was accused of having gunned down several of those responsible for unhappiness, Mathias Olbane had vehemently denied being a member of a terrorist organization. Despite the judge's sarcasm, he insisted obstinately that he was a writer and that he lived by his pen. *An Autumn at the Boyols'* and *Splendor of the Skiff* had been produced for the court, but several paragraphs, which admittedly had nothing syrupy, nothing ambiguous, and nothing kind to say about the world of real capitalism, were considered clear calls to political murder and were retained as corroborating evidence.

The condemned was twenty-four. Twenty-six years later, after receiving a two-year reduction in his sentence for good behavior, Mathias Olbane left the penitentiary, didn't look back at the gigantic doors that closed behind him, and fell ill. The autoimmune oncoglyphosis erupted a week after his release.

During his long stay behind bars, Mathias Olbane didn't write novels, didn't write short stories, didn't compose poems. Instead, he assigned himself a literary task that revisited his first poetic attempts and magnified them, resulting in a vast and evidently very powerful original work. He invented words and maniacally organized them by categories. Telling stories no longer held any interest for him whatsoever. He contemplated the clouds that meandered beyond the bars and the window guards, he let his gaze wander across the grey and dreary décor of his cell and along the disheartening silhouettes of his companions when, in certain years, they brought cellmates into his small space. He reflected on the echoes that reached him from the outside, on the precious and often unverifiable morsels that told him that the world was still headed for the worst. He listened to the complaints or the songs of the other prisoners. It was his life. But the idea of reproducing it with words didn't appeal to him, and even less so the thought of developing a fiction that would start with all this as a backdrop and loosely take it further.

When he had paper and something to write with, which wasn't always the case in some of the prisons where they transferred him, he formulated lists of imaginary terms, such as names of plants, names of persecuted or exterminated peoples, or quite simply made-up names of camp victims. As the years passed, these lists accumulated and formed thick bundles, which he dreamily flipped through without ever rereading, and to which he was not at all attached, only protesting on principle when they confiscated them, or accepting their loss during the transfers. Since he did not consult them in case of doubt and since any archives that he could have preserved unfailingly ended up disappearing, these long series of neologisms included repetitions, recurrences, and duplicates. To estimate their length with precision would be a task as thankless as it would be absurd. Nonetheless, taking the spirit of Mathias Olbane's system and the time he had available to him as a starting point, we can confirm without risk of excessive error that after twenty-six years in captivity, he had forged approximately a hundred thousand words, divided as follows:

- sixty thousand first and last names of victims of unhappiness
- twenty thousand names of imaginary plants, mushrooms, and herbs
- ten thousand names of places, rivers, and localities
- and ten thousand various words that do not belong to any language, but that have a certain phonetic logic that makes them sound familiar.

That's what Mathias Olbane's work consisted of.

Without eliciting notable anger from him, his fellow inmates would sometimes help themselves to a few pages of the manuscript to use as toilet paper, and even he, though only in the event of a serious shortage, would put the beginning or the end of a list to similar use. Even in the years when he was alone, as the overpopulation of prisons saw ups and downs, he wasn't reluctant to reach down from his seat on the malodorous bucket, towards one of his numerous and monstrous directories, and without bemoaning it whatsoever, tear out a page to wipe himself. He had never considered his creative activities to be sacred; poetry seemed dead to him from the moment it landed in the ink of a poem, and at any rate, he didn't consider this vast enterprise of neology as exhibiting the slightest connection to what, in the outside world, one still called art or literature.

When, on the day he got his freedom, the guards invited him to pack up his vast manuscripts, his notebooks, and his piles of paper filled with tiny, compact handwriting, he gestured contemptuously and abandoned the whole thing next to the bucket. He explained to these men, who had ended up respecting him or at least accepting him as one accepts a half-wit or a harmless crackpot, that he preferred, once on the outside, to start fresh, and to finally give a satisfying form to what the guards and even he, out of laziness, called his dictionaries.

He was out of prison, and contrary to his promises, he hadn't resumed his lexicological activities, he hadn't started his dictionaries again from scratch. He could have taken advantage, in his own way, of his newfound freedom, he could have plunged into the austere life of a creator, not unlike the one he led in prison but without the bars, and he had vaguely envisioned living the remainder of his days in an exile without pathos, a peaceful solitude, balanced, devoid of bitterness, but he hadn't yet had the time to carry out this humble dream, and his life took an unexpected turn. The autoimmune oncoglyphosis had struck one week after his liberation, and it had cast him, with no transition, immediately and irretrievably, into the world of freaks and invalids. Thanks to a sister who remained relatively loyal to him, and who, more out of a sense of obligation than kindheartedness, had dipped into her meager savings so that he could have a roof over his head and basic medical assistance, he had been admitted into this rest house, separated from the world, where he would survive or where he would die.

His sister's husband, a very old friend from his guerrilla days, hadn't had to go to too much trouble to procure a pistol and a few bullets for him. This was a man who was now halfheartedly defending social democracy, but who still had old anarchist leanings and contacts with arms dealers. He suspected that Mathias Olbane wouldn't fire at anyone besides himself, and for a number of reasons, that didn't bother him. On the contrary, he hoped for it. As for Mathias Olbane's sister, she knew about the pistol. When she was helping Mathias Olbane to gather up his belongings to leave, she found the weapon wrapped in a cloth, but she had wrapped it back up without saying anything. She would have protested if anyone had accused her of encouraging her brother's self-destructive plans and, even in talking with her husband, she wouldn't have admitted it, but she too thought that Mathias Olbane ought to soon disappear. A quarter-century earlier, she had admired him with affection, and before his trial and for many months after the verdict she had regularly gone to visit him, but then he was transferred to a penitentiary five thousand kilometers away and she could no longer tangibly maintain their relationship. And years went by, by the handful, by the half-dozen, by the dozen, and while she was being crushed by her own life, by her life as a supermarket cashier, she had given up thinking of him as a living person. And now he had re-emerged into the normal world, arriving as though from another planet, terrible to look at, with no means of supporting himself and with nothing to look forward to besides physical degradation and a mass grave. For everyone, the evidence was clear: he no longer had any place in the world and he needed to be done with it. Carrying on with his life had made sense during all his years of imprisonment, for he had at least had the goal of one day crossing over to the other side of the walls, but now that he was on the outside, his horizon had retracted too much for him to have a reason to suppress his death wish.

In the depths of the darkness, Mathias Olbane concentrated on not mixing up his count. He counted slowly. The pistol weighed heavily in his right hand. He didn't think about how stale his relationship with his sister had become, or his brother-in-law's cynical eagerness to put a Makarov in his hand just like the one he had used to slaughter public enemies. He deliberately thought as little as possible. He endeavored not to botch his laborious counting. Sometimes, by some automatism that he obviously couldn't control, he surprised himself by mentally tabulating a new list. He no longer felt he had to preserve, pursue, or complete his unattainable repertoire of imaginary words, but the habit was so firmly anchored in him that, under the rhythm imposed by the monotone succession of numbers, he was pierced at every moment by the almost musical temptation to create, at each multiple of ten, for instance, a name of a character, a victim, or an animal. He was wary of this possible diversion and fought it. He didn't wish to be distracted, he obstinately willed himself not to awaken anything within him besides the shadowy present, and once again, he noticed that his mind was fixated on a banal sequence from the distant past, on a contemptible scene, a moment of doing laundry in his cell when the worn-out shirt finally tore, or a brawl in the showers, or the arbitrary confiscation of two notebooks during a search. Now's the time, he thought. I have to do it. It'll hardly take any effort. Then he heard himself panting, and, still counting and counting, he inspected the imprecise image of his head that the mirror sent back to him, and he heard the faint crackling sounds, the dreadful crackling that the skin of his skull emitted when it swallowed his hair. He didn't pull the trigger.

And so the nights passed without result. They were torrid. When it rained, the open window let in the din of the storm. The noise was overbearing, it dominated and even canceled out all the other sounds outside as well as inside the room. So these were hours when he could plant himself in front of the mirror without this sizzling of his skull, his dermis, and his distress.

But when it didn't rain, he heard the sizzling all the time.

His lips moved in the darkness, and most of the time he couldn't make out his mouth in the mirror, or he could vaguely see it, just as he had a hard time distinguishing the reflection of the pistol whose barrel was wedged between his jaws, right where his molars were missing. It was too dark. When he passed two hundred and fifty, the rest of the numbers seemed more and more nerve-wracking to him, and despite his best efforts, he started to think more about his anguish than about the steady, tragic accumulation, and he lost his way among his thoughts along the short path that remained for him to walk before his death. He suddenly hesitated on the section he was on and let himself be pulled along towards the parasitic discourses on himself. New icy streams of sweat zigzagged across his back, under his thighs, and all over his face. He felt the trickles form and he knew that his sweat wasn't the only liquid to well up from his flesh. Repugnant fluids spread across the surface of his physiognomy, less liquidy than the most natural brine, and beaded up on his forehead, soaked his eyebrows, rolled down his eyelids and the bridge of his nose, dampened his temples, his cheekbones and his nape, his chin. Once in a while, as he approached the endpoint, the thought flashed through his head that he was a circus freak, someone whom no living being could look at in peace, and so he would abruptly stop his counting, stricken, aware that his posture in front of the mirror, his slow emptying of numbers, his endless wait had something pathetic and even ridiculous about them. He sighed, clouded over even more than before, no longer thinking of anything, no longer knowing where he was in his backwards count. He wiped his weapon and his hands on his pajama top, on his striped pants, on his breast pocket. The bloody dew that escaped from his skin made him gag. He couldn't see it, but he could imagine the appearance, the viscosity, and it made him gag.

Then he started his miserable count back at zero.

When he reached the number four hundred and forty-four, he let a few more seconds pass, then he opened the dresser drawer, he wrapped the pistol in the undershirt that served as a case, he closed the drawer again, and, since once again he hadn't managed to kill himself, he got up, went to bed, and tried to fall back to sleep.

SHE STANDS UNDER the barred window, she doesn't look at the sky, she leans back against the cement well, she cries. She is a magnificent woman. She cries, there isn't the slightest difference between us, nothing will ever be able to separate us, neither time nor space, I cry with her. Twelve years ago, she killed men who deserved to be reduced to nothing, men who had been everything, or, at least, quite a lot, she killed enemies of the people that many would have liked to kill if they had had the courage, but very few people have the courage to carry out justice, almost nobody engages in vengeance and retaliation in the name of the people. But she did it. She assassinated, as I would have liked to, assassins who had indirectly killed hundreds of thousands and even millions of people. She was arrested and sentenced to life, she was locked up in an isolated correctional facility, and in the circles that decide the fate of the defeated, it was said that she was dead, they hoped she would die, but she held on, perhaps because she had the advantage of particularly resistant genetic traits, difficult to destroy, or because she had in mind the end goal of our organization, or perhaps because they forgot to send killers to her to take care of the problem once and for all, and also because the guards were afraid of her.

She is a magnificent woman.

She is locked in a cell of miserly dimensions, and has had no companions for eight years already. She can't take it anymore. She has mutilated herself multiple times during the preceding years, especially during winter when the prison is cold and damp and when the idea of living and hanging on dissolves. Mentally, she has lost much of her confidence. She is unwell. She likes to lean back against the wall and imagine that she is passing through the wall, that her hair is disheveled by the wind, that she is beneath the shifting skies of the steppe, in the middle of shifting grasses, and that she speaks louder than the gusts of wind, that she speaks the world. When the penitential administration authorizes her to have some paper and a ballpoint pen, she speaks the world in written form, using abbreviations and an encrypted language to which she alone holds the keys, and when she has constructed a story, she whispers it again and again crouching or lying in front of the door, she speaks to the corridor, to the draft whistling through the empty floor. She occupies cell number 1614 and, since the death of Maria Iguacel in the adjacent cell, she no longer has anyone to talk to.

Nonetheless, several times a week, she speaks the world. She invents dreams, she retells stories that she has written, or she reflects on our battles, those we have led dressed as warriors and those we have led dressed as prisoners and that we continue to lead with the word, breaths, hallucinations, and I don't know what else that is much too serene to be hatred. Oftentimes she will also pay homage to those who have been assassinated, as we all do at some point or another in our long days. Then she will repeat a narract, a lesson, or an excerpt of a romånce that she didn't compose herself, but that circulated through the prison and that the imprisoned men and women, to fend off forgetfulness and out of love, have learned by heart. Most of the time, she imagines that she has her arms outstretched to better feel the wind of the steppe, to better enfold the universe of grasses and sky, and that in front of her are gathered a few sympathetic nomads, or wandering souls wrapped in bandages, just barely having escaped the ovens of hell, or black crows possessed by shamans. She imagines this audience, our audience, and she speaks the world, and speaking the world, she talks about us.

Her name is Linda Woo. If you want to imagine her features and her appearance, you might think of a film from Hong Kong. She looks like Dora Kwok in *Lonely Dragons*. In fact, she's even more beautiful, for passion has left its mark on her face, the fire of the struggle of the just against the monsters. Behind the mask of pain and solitude, beneath the skin that has become ugly from lack of sunlight, a light persists that nothing can extinguish. Like us, she has lost all battles. She is magnificent, but she has lost. And now, illuminated from within, she hums against the wall, she softly knocks the back of her skull against the wall, and already she is there, in the blast of wind, and she whispers a speech to the nomads and to the dead. And today she pays homage to the inmate from the neighboring cell, to Maria

Iguacel, it's a lesson that she utters, one of the small hallucinated forms that the post-exotic writers call a lesson.

She takes on the voice of Maria Iguacel. Suddenly she is Maria Iguacel. So am I.

"The post-exotic writers," she begins.

Her voice doesn't carry far because of the opposing wind. Rasping grasses whose name she doesn't know blow right up against her legs, and not even a hundred yards from there, she glimpses a first listener approaching, a fat guy from out of nowhere who looks like a huge dead man, asleep and bad-tempered. He doesn't look at her, and, moreover, he has neither eyes nor a face. She doesn't know his name, either. She supposes that he can't hear her well, and perhaps that he can't hear her at all, but, at first, she speaks especially to him:

"If the post-exotic writers used to involve themselves in politics and literature, it wasn't to try and obtain more comfortable personal lives, or because they wanted to approach those who, with a flashy humility, seem to be above the world and who govern and order it, or because they want to enjoy the right to speak in the name of masters and in defense of masters, in exchange for the right to expect their flattery, the little pats on the back, the treats and trinkets that the powerful hand out to their servants, whether they are politicians or artists. No, they didn't want to purr from baseness and rub affectionately against the masters' boots while imagining that they had freely chosen to be domesticated, all while their presence near the boots was always the result of the masters' choice among those who were educated according to their masters' logic. No, we must look for the roots of their engagement elsewhere. We must define our desires in another way."

She catches her breath. She waits a few dozen seconds. The grasses blow around her, the plumes sway at the top of the long stalks. The wind smells like peat. After the fat dead man, two burn victims, arisen from the intermediate world, make a brief appearance, then sit down in a hollow in the landscape and can no longer be seen. Far in the distance, several kilometers away, three nomads on horseback advance slowly next to their herd. Nobody listens to her. She speaks to some and then to others, to those who have disappeared and to those who are enormously far away, she talks to them as though they were right up close to her and very attentive.

"The post-exotic writers, she says, Myriam Ossorgone, Maria Clementi, Jean Doïvode, Irina Kobayashi, Jean Edelman, Maria Schrag, and many others, were involved in politics to attempt to completely overturn everything that had been established on the planet as though permanently, everything that fostered eternal unhappiness and forced five billion human wretches to live in the muck, in the dust, and the absence of hope. They arose to destroy the roots and seeds of unhappiness, and, early on, to be finished with the masters and with the masters' dogs. The post-exotic writers weren't mere scribblers of rubbish, they were armed and engaged in politics, they had taken the road of secrecy and subversion, and with no fear either of madness or of death, they threw themselves into a battle that they had but the faintest chance of winning, an infinitesimal chance, and thus they found themselves soldiers and loners, laughably few at the front of a war in which, combat after combat, they lost everything. It even happened that they lost the certainty that one day the wretches' children would open their eyes on a world not filled with shadows, not ruled by the mafia, and not unequal. But they did not bend, they continued to fight, counting the dead men and women and refusing to betray them, refusing all perspective of capitulation and refusing to give up their weapons, and, when the ideological and military encirclement was too fierce to allow for the possibility that they would live in freedom, they refused to change their tune before the enemy or to lower their sights, which naturally drove them into the hallways of death or into the hallways of houses of arrest where they were locked up like one locks up harmful mutant animals that are incapable of submission."

She is out of breath. The wind tears the words from her mouth. On her passionate, magnificent face, tears flow. She doesn't fold her arms to wipe them away. She is in a trance, but her body is threatening at each moment to betray her, to collapse or to tear apart, and she knows that it's best to move as little as possible. It's best to freeze in order to keep going. She is beneath the sky, facing the sky, in the midst of the grasses. The nomads in the distance have slipped into a valley with their herd. She no longer sees them. Of her audience, only the burn victims have remained within the sound of her voice. The fat, graceless dead man listened to her for a moment, then he drew apart and, after a hundred meters or so, he plunged into a field of reeds and didn't return. Crows hop between the gray-green, gray-yellow tufts, grasses with a Mongol name, and, hardly unfolding their wings, they go to inspect the state of the burn victims in the hollow of the ditch, then they return and set themselves up on the grassy crest. It's for them, too, that Linda Woo gives her lesson.

"There you have what political engagement means for us," she says.

When Linda Woo cries, I cry too. But it matters little. We are not here to pity ourselves.

"Post-exoticism's writers," she begins again, "have in their memory, without exception, the wars and the ethnic and social exterminations that were carried out from one end of the 20th century to the other, they forget none and pardon none, they also keep permanently in mind the savageries and the inequalities that are exacerbated among men, and not for a second do they listen to the masters' dogs that suggest that they adapt their propaganda to reality and to the present, in other words to the present and to the reality as those responsible for unhappiness conceive of them, and that advise them to break with obsolete beliefs, to admit defeat, and to join once again, after, of course, the formalities of prison release, the ranks of the official lyricists, where they could participate in turn and in their own way in the philosophical and poetic beautification of unhappiness, for instance in singing the advantages of the present and in explaining, to the countless wretches on this planet, that everything will be fine for them, or rather for their descendants, if they are patient, if they are willing to vegetate for another thousand years without laying a finger on anything. The post-exotic writers turn their backs on these advisers who smell of the same odors as the masters. They consider that the 20th century was made up of of ten decades of large-scale pain, and that the 21st century has started down the same route, for the objective causes and the responsible parties of this pain are still there, and have even reinforced and reproduced themselves, like in an endless middle age."

Linda Woo pauses for a moment. She doesn't feel well, facing the wind, against the wall, in the steppe where distances give her vertigo, in the cell where she can't take three steps without bumping into something infinitely hard and impenetrable.

She wants to scream.

She has a cry in her throat, but in the end, she murmurs:

"That is what motivates our confinement in a radical thought of revolt."

She closes her eyes. Nobody knows what she sees. Nobody knows if the crows peck in front of her, in the ditch, or if they have flown away, nor if the dead are still there, covered in burnt bandages, nor whether they listen to her. Nobody knows what can be heard. Wind under the infinite sky? … A lesson from Linda Woo? … Or a lesson from Maria Iguacel? … Or a gust of wind through the empty floor? …

"Once they have been crushed and condemned," she begins again, "post-exoticism's writers persist in their existence, in isolation in high-security quarters or in permanent monastic cloisters of death. Their breath has no longer served to ensure their survival as useless bodies, let's say as lungs with consciousness, as talkative lungs. Their memory has become a collection of dreams. Their murmurs have ended up fashioning collective books with no clear claims of author-ship. They have set themselves to ruminating on promises not kept and they have invented worlds where failure is as systematic and as stinging as it is in what you call the real world."

She interrupts herself. The wind around her no longer disturbs the grasses, everything is immobile, even the crows. She would none-theless like to see those are lying or perhaps seated in front of her, invisible in the hole in the earth, the burn victims who must still be there, but who show no signs of themselves.

"In what the dead call the real world," she clarifies.

She spends a moment reflecting, then she feels that her back is against the wall and she releases her head against the cement, she caresses the cement once or twice with the back of her skull, then she swings her head back harder, until she hears the impact and feels pain. She knows that from now on she will have to go faster so that she doesn't lose the thread of her speech.

"The dead," she stutters.

She is in pain, the solitude injures her horribly.

She cries. I cry with her.

"Their word has rung through a space where the living are scarce," she says with difficulty. "In this way, and in only this way, should post-exotic literature be seen: as a final useless and imaginary testimony spoken by the exhausted or by the dead and for the dead. Our word."

Time passes.

"Of course," she begins again, "our word does not purport to have any usefulness whatsoever in the concrete egalitarian combat that we ought to be leading, beyond the walls, to liberate from cycles of unhappiness the five or six billion people who are submerged in it. We know that. We don't entertain any illusion about that."

She doesn't move for a moment, then she bashes her skull, several times, against the cement wall that she is leaning against.

"We have no pride in wielding the word, even if we know that our poetry is not comparable to the servile juggling that the talkative domestics of the masters produce in abundance. We know our insignificance. In a universe where the multiplication of the word is the loam on which the actors of unhappiness prosper, on this ignoble theatrical stage where the profusion of contradictory debates is a cynical screen behind which the masters keep their hands free, the word has neither influence nor strength. We no longer live in this universe, but our imprisoning fortress is also not a place where saying things allows you to change things. The post-exotic word will interrupt itself when the last of our writers is extinguished, and nobody anywhere will realize it. Still, as long as a little breath remains in us, we will invent more and more of the absurd magic of this word, we will go into the words and we will speak the world.

Linda Woo is in shreds, wind and solitude have torn her apart once again, she is drenched in sweat and tears. Me too.

"The lesson is finished," she says, to conclude.

HE REMEMBERS the gray light that filled the courtyard beyond the classroom's high windows, he remembers the persistent smell of pee that hovered around his classmates and that perhaps was due more to the poorly washed floor and the sticky dampness of the desks than to the undergarments and childish incontinence of the students, he remembers the agreeable friction, the light granulation of the paper under the lead of his pencil, he remembers the sense of a fever than ran through his cheeks and upper body, the sense of urgency, of desire, of imperious need, he remembers that the teacher passed very close to him and watched him, but without comment, without bothering him, aware that he had broken through the moorings of scholastic discipline, that he was no longer listening, that he was no longer leaning on the required exercises, aware deep down that something extraordinary was happening and that it was better to respect the flow of it, for it's unusual that a five-year-old boy, barely literate, escapes all institutional constraint in such an open way, unfolds the inside of a notebook cover, and starts to pour out a story unlike any other, and he remembers that after having blackened the interior space, the virgin space of a first notebook cover, after having filled it with his awkward, wobbly, disorderly handwriting, he seized a second notebook cover, then a third, determined to pursue his composition whatever the cost, suddenly no longer obeying the instructions or conventions, freeing himself from all authority, and first and foremost neglecting the authority of the teacher who grazed him and who paused above him for a beat, curious to see what he was doing, for he was jealously concentrated on his task, engrossed in the effort that his narration demanded, and he also remembers the images that formed and crystalized in his mind, the dialogues of adults that took place there and that he didn't know how to transcribe, he remembers the jungle, the forest, the clouds that seemed to reflect the fires, he remembers the animals, the cries, the children who ran, terrorized, dressed in tattered oversized jackets, and he remembers the heat that pricked his eyes, the hot passion that he tried to overpower by forming the letters as quickly as possible and by lining up words that he had never used until then, for he was still very little, in a phase of his existence where everything was new, speech, emotions, images, dreams and reality, knowledge, and in fact he remembers the impression of naive triumph that brought him towards the idea that he had just entered into the world of stories that one invents oneself, and also the idea that he was creating a more complex text than he should have been able to naturally at his age, and for that he felt a clearly proud joy, and also he remembers that he had decided not to stop when faced with the obstacles that written language accumulated beneath his fingers and to keep in mind that the top priority wasn't to execute feats of perfect spelling to please the teacher but to lay down the text torrentially, to lay it down ignoring all other considerations, to make it exist despite the abrasion of standards and the grammatical approximations that he suspected would be numerous, and moreover he didn't have an inward goal of offering up this text for the reading pleasure of adults, and even less, of course, as reading material for his classmates, most of whom still had trouble deciphering words of more than two syllables, and he remembers, too, that this certitude of making the text exist for himself, of working for no audience, that this conviction had given him strength from the moment he had begun to spread himself on the pages of the first notebook cover, and also he remembers that this happened in October, and that in the courtyard, while the morning light was growing steadier, a peculiar rain started up, a gossamer rain, like there used to be ages ago, in autumn, a soft rain, or more like a snow composed of thousands of long webs from minuscule spiders, and at the same time he remembers the name of the teacher and of a few of his classmates, mainly girls, and in response to the question that he was just asked again by a scratchy, crazed voice, and which was accompanied by a smack to the head, he says:

"I don't remember. I don't remember anything. My mind is empty."

Several seconds of incredulity follow on the part of his interrogators, then another slap, this time right in the face.

There are two of them, a man and a woman, and they take turns. After the slap, the woman repeats the question in a shrill voice. The interrogation started ten minutes ago. It is being led in violation of all common sense. What do they want to make him confess? He can't figure it out and he concerns himself with it as little as possible. He's in their hands and he doesn't want to cooperate, he has never cooperated with inquisitors, and even if these ones are more or less his own kind, even if they belong as he does to a category that is intellectually, socially, and concretely wretched and rotten, he returns to his old tactics of dissidence. He pretends to understand nothing, but moreover, he forces himself to understand nothing so that his idiocy takes on greater authenticity. He tries to feel profoundly passive and stupid. He remains in the presence of screaming and mistreatment, of course he can't deny that, but at the same time he floats at a distance from the real, at a distance from everything. He has turned inward where possible, in one of his latest moments of fear, perhaps not very solid but very far from the present and even from the past, he has taken refuge in a moment from his childhood. Ages ago, he perfected this technique of intimate evasion, he put it into practice when he found himself in police stations, he continued to adopt it during his trials, in front of his judges, then much later in the presence of psychiatrists, and now that he's confronted by his insane comrades, by his insane comrades who have gone on a rampage, he figures that it's better to barricade himself there once again, in the depths, at the source, far from the atrocious world of adults. People rough him up, people want to make him talk, want him to tell them what they want to hear. He lets them beat him and get angry, he floats elsewhere, in a secret piece of elsewhere, he drifts there, in an elementary school classroom, far away.

He remembers that, while with his left hand he held steady the notebook cover he was writing in, he sensed in the background, around him, the rest of the class, hardly more than twenty-five children, twenty-six or twenty-seven perhaps, but fewer than thirty, among them Linda Woo, Eliane Schust, Mourma Yogodane, his three girlfriends, accomplices in the schoolyard and accomplices in the cabinets, as well as little Jean Doïevode, son of the man who was shot, sitting right behind him, a smart kid despite his age, six years old tops, never out of ideas for phantasmagoric or subversive plots, but who was quietly dozing off that day, no doubt drugged by the thick October air, by the silence of this October morning, and, if he sensed the nearby presence of beings who were a part of his life, of his friends, he also felt on him the weight of the teacher's surveillance, for even if she had accepted his plunge into writing, into his written exploration of a parallel universe where school no longer existed, even if she had judged it wise not to intervene, she was careful not to let her deviant attitude be remarked, and not to let it drag the other students into his no-man's-land, and he also remembers the color of the sky beyond the window, a color of sad wool, a sky that still seemed heavy with the morning's fog, with a hint of azure that timidly pierced the gloom, and he remembers the gossamer threads, the rippling filaments, the hairs of such extreme fineness that they could not be seen if backlit, but whose silvery whiteness would stand out in perfect clarity when they floated in front of the leaves of the trees in the courtyard, when they slowly flew in front of the chestnut and linden trees, he remembers that for an instant he almost let himself be distracted by the silky texture of the air outside, by this miraculous rain, for, while burning with a violent excitement that demanded he neglect any mental activity besides writing, he still held an interest in the strange things of the world, in the supernatural phenomena against which adults' confidence would waver, and the autumnal apparition of the gossamer was among these, about which some had told him that they were traces of a migration of microscopic spiders, while others hesitated, then spoke more willingly of the hair of angels and associating their sudden, massive appearance with the passage, in the smallest hours of the night, of cosmic vessels that had come from who knows which constellations, inhabited by creatures that had no wish to forge relationships with humans and subhumans but that observed them and judged them, while still others, like Jean Doïevode's mother, reported that scholars disagreed on the subject, that some had determined that the origin of the angels' hair was certainly vegetal, not animal, thereby eliminating the spider hypothesis, and that furthermore Lamarck's theory hadn't really been refuted, in which he maintained that what we had here was a sort of crystallization of droplets of fog, for it was true that once they touched the ground the threads quickly dissipated, evaporated, sublimated, and so he remembers that for an instant, instead of being completely inhabited by the images that his mind and his fingers did their best to translate, with only a child's words, he had been tempted to lift his head to follow the evolutions of this ghostly cloud, but that the next moment he easily resisted the temptation, and that he returned to his writerly work, and he also remembers the sentence that he was finishing at the exact moment when his concentration briefly waned, he sees in front of him again his rough handwriting, the lines that refused to keep their horizontality, he feels again the faint warmth of the soft pencil, black, around which he clenched his fingers, and the feeling of pride and inevitability that burned in the backs of his eye sockets, as though embers glowed beneath his skull, he leans anew on the cardboard-colored paper, yellower, in any case, than the paper inside his notebook, thicker, and he effortlessly reads this bit of text, *Sudenly they herd eeeeeoooooooooeeeeeeoooooo it was the red poleece who were leaving the forest with the lion the boa the giant turtel and suddenly they saw the plane that had flied that morning and that disapeered and the red poleece had told them that the wite poleece had killd all the forest aminals all the children and the ants told them that the plane had drownded in the see that was stormy,* he remembers this sentence and the images that jostled in his mind, and the warm intoxication that flowed through him at the thought that he was in the midst of writing a story, of writing what had to be written in exactly the way it had to be written, he remembers this satisfaction that accompanied him even while he was writing laboriously, choppily, because his fingers hadn't yet mastered the elementary reflexes and codes, he remembers this intimate boastfulness that was superimposed on the artisanal pleasure of composing and that warmed him, and the inexplicable feeling that he was examining himself from the exterior, sympathetically, from on high, like an adult could have done, like the teacher, for instance, must have done when she froze over his shoulder, for he heard her walk up behind him and stop, and he remembered the teacher's name, which had been in shadows until now, Madame Mohndjee, Frau Mohndjee, and he said:

"I can't answer you. My memory is empty. They emptied my

memory with their electric shocks. I no longer have any memories at all."

Once again they beat him. A deluge of punches, slaps, kicks in the shins, the calves. He goes from one side to the other, they've tied him to a wheelchair, he can't dodge anything, they push him up against the wall, they abandon him, they start up again. They've slipped into white coats that they have stolen from medical personnel, but even with closed eyes, you couldn't mistake them for psychiatrists, or even police officers disguised as psychiatrists. Their odor, their wild eyes, and their nervousness betray them. They are nothing but two mental patients who have seized power in the special penitentiary clinic. Their sole authority is that of violence. They are determined to get him to confess that he has contacts with parallel universes, with aliens, that since his birth he has been a double agent, that he pretends to be insane like them, that he knows the list of the next to be struck down, that when he wrote books he inserted secret orders into all the chapters, invitations to a secret and criminal practice of patience, they want him to recognize that he prepares the transformation of humans into spiders. This is the sort of misdeed that they wait for him to confess. All of this is accompanied by mental confusion, by whispered asides and muttering, which makes the interrogation indistinct and even grotesque. He knows that they were brought in on charges of violent insanity, that they are murderous, uncontrollable, and since the beginning, he resigned himself to consider that, like them, he has experienced one more painful phase in his interminable journey of imprisonment and hospitalization, and that, even if everything suggests that this will be the last, it's better not to attach too much importance to it.

The man in the white coat was condemned for a series of political assassinations that he carried out in his youth, and was then transferred, after twenty-eight years of high-security prison, into the world of special psychiatry. He is fifty-seven and he will never again leave this establishment unless it's in a coffin. He hasn't understood a thing about the outside world in a long time, his mental filters are encrusted with grime and no longer send him anything to interpret his surroundings besides motifs of rage and dread. After having made himself master of the place and having slit the throats of the medical actors who, according to him, intended to exterminate all of the residents and replace them with clay statues, he decided not to continue his evasion, contenting himself instead with tasks of immediate management. He delegated the responsibilities of defending the building to a team of experienced cannibals. As for him, he oversees sorting the survivors, leads the interrogation of suspects, and pronounces summary judgments. His roommates are the most threatened, for he's had years to learn not to trust them. He's already eliminated two of them. His name is Bruno Khatchatourian. The shaved spots for the electroshocks are visible on his skull.

The woman in the white coat is named Greta, nobody knows her last name. She's a relatively new resident, her stay at the special hospital began ten months ago, but she's been here long enough to gain Bruno Khatchatourian's trust, enough, at least, for him to become her lover and listen with sullen enthusiasm to her suggestions of murder. She was sentenced for horrible attacks; she couldn't integrate into the normal correctional environment and the prisons finally washed their hands of her by entrusting her to the special doctors. The personnel often claimed that she was the most dangerous patient in the women's wing, and that her moments of apparent tranquility hid a cunning fury, ready to overflow at the first opportunity. Greta actively helped Bruno Khatchatourian and several others in the bloodiest episodes of the insurrection that has just taken place. She now presides over the operations of sorting and investigation, slapping her own aberrant accusations on top of Bruno Khatchatourian's suspicious constructions. Her hair must have been a beautiful raven black once, but now it flies in every direction when she agitates and gesticulates, and a good deal of black has ceded its place to a dirty gray, disagreeable, almost powdery.

In the chief doctor's ravaged office, above the bodies of the doctor, the doctor's assistant, and two guards, the dialogue between Greta and Bruno Khatchatourian begins again. Both of them use a nightmarish tone, and sometimes they stammer, overwhelmed by tics, by their internal fears that they refuse to express and that twist their mouths, ravaged also by their poor knowledge of the ins and outs of their own discourse. There are even moments when they lose the thread to such an extent that they forget they're in the middle of investigating the morality of one of their toughest co-detainees.

"First of all, the moon must not go down," says Greta.

"Which?" asks Bruno Khatchatourian.

"The moon," says Greta. "The night moon. It must not go down. It didn't catch fire. The stinking moon."

The one that stinks like the old dairy farm," Bruno Khatchatourian confirms.

"Yes, like the old dairy farm," exults Greta. "The old cow pails, the leeches in the ditch. They've tried everything. It didn't catch fire. It doesn't smell like fire. It never smelled like fire."

"And when it's gone down?" stammers Bruno Khatchatourian.

"It won't go down!" Greta says angrily. "It stinks! It stinks like old lady Philippe's apron!"

"That old bitch," hazards Bruno Khatchatourian. "It must not go down!"

"You don't understand," Greta sneers. "Old lady Philippe's apron. That bitch's apron. If she waves it under our noses, we're fucked!"

They get closer to him. They jostle him. Bruno Khatchatourian hits him on the chest. He takes a boxer's stance, reels troublingly, seems to concentrate in order to drive a final, terrible strike into his solar plexus, but in the end, he misses.

"And you," he asks his prisoner, "Do you know her, old lady Philippe?"

"Nobody knows her," says Greta. She's the one who killed me, that bitch. When I was little. She had made a pact with the authorities. She shook her apron under my nose."

"This guy, he knows her," suggests Bruno Khatchatourian.

Greta paces the room. Her hair flies around her.

"She killed me, that old bitch," she repeats. She shook her nasty old apron under my nose. I was so young. She was with the others. They all killed me."

"This guy, too, he made a pact with the authorities," Bruno Khatchatourian takes up again.

He accompanies his affirmation with a kick to the wheelchair.

The chair slides half a meter, it's going to hit the wall. The prisoner lets out a groan.

"We're going to waste him," Greta promises. "We won't even wait for the moon to go down or not. Then we can kill the ones that are left, and my parents, and ... My parents, those bastards ... They made a pact with old lady Philippe. They're just like him ... We'll kill them all!"

"He teamed up with our parents," mumbles Bruno Khatchatourian. "With the dark forces. With the demons."

"With the demons that piss on the moon," Greta finishes. "With the capitalist demons and the demons that stink."

"Will you confess, yes or no?" screams Bruno Khatchatourian.

"With the capitalists, with old lady Philippe," Greta roars.

They come back to him, they beat him.

He accepts the bad luck cheerfully, and he waits, almost tranquilly, for their rage to reach a new level and for them to waste him. He knows the end is near, and rather than taking stock of his existence, rather than invoking the last decade passed in exile, marked by a long, monotonous chain of fights and days of prostration, or what preceded the universe of special medicine, a life of guerrilla warfare, unpublished or badly published novels, and confinement in a high-security neighborhood, he prefers to take refuge in Frau Mohndjee's classroom.

An October morning.

The daylight that remains in the courtyard like an unfinished dawn.

A gray day, bluish gray.

The odor of his classmates' pee, the whiffs of pee and mops that swirl around the desks, around the floor that's washed every evening and that, in autumn, doesn't dry.

Behind the windowpanes, thousands of mysterious filaments that drift in the absence of wind.

Madame Mohndjee, Frau Mohndjee who walks up and down the aisles separating the students, who dictates elementary calculations to her students and who carefully ensures his neighbors don't distract him, who scolds Jean Doïevode when he starts to fidget behind him, who even borrows a fourth notebook cover from among Jean Doïevode's belongings and places it next to him, so that he can continue his work uninterrupted.

He remembers this initial session of literary creation, he remembers that in the first notebook cover he had written the number One and that he had added a title, Begining, having the hazy intuition that a day would come when the question of the ending would be asked, but later, much later, and about that he remembers this intense feeling of no return that propelled him forward, that authorized him or rather forced him to reject the law of the group, the law of the class, and instead of doing calculation exercises with the others, pushed him to fill a third, then a fourth notebook cover, and he remembers that the moment he numbered them, then, when he smoothed them with the palm of his hand before pouring out text, he was filled with a wave of exaltation due very clearly to the fact that he was hereby adding a new tome to the work that he had undertaken, to this work that seemed immense to him, and he remembers that as he began writing the fourth volume, and while the intoxication grew stronger, he had encountered the questioning gaze of Mourma Yogodane, and that he had returned to his task without responding, and of Mourma Yogodane he remembers the contact of her teeth on his tongue, because far from the adults, in a sphere entirely real but private, unknown to adults, the children of Frau Mohndjee's class surrendered regularly to sexual experiences, several children anyway, who made up a small clique in which he was included, composed primarily of Mourma Yogodane, Jean Doïevode, Linda Woo, and Eliane Schust, and he remembered that from time to time they closed themselves into the cabinets and that there they developed, moreover without emotion, the foundation of their childlike eroticism, without emotion and simply with curiosity, above all with the impression of accomplishing something that was necessary but that didn't do much for them, perhaps aside from the minor euphoria of having acted like adults away from the adults, and suddenly he remembers at once the sexuality of the cabinets and the sentence with which he started the third volume of his work, Twelve years later they comed back they bringed some poizened food to kill the boa the giant turtel *and the marshuns and they seed that the trees around the village was red and that in the streets the poleece was ded the marshuns killd them,* he remembers at once the faulty spelling of this childish phrase, word for word, and the contact of Mourma Yogodane's teeth with his tongue, for one of the clandestine activities to which they devoted themselves in the cabinets consisted of licking one another's teeth, each one in turn and with no other pleasure than that of a job completed, and he remembers other practices that didn't elicit their enthusiasm either and in which they cavorted in silence, not moving any more than was necessary and without the thought occurring to them that they were breaking prohibitions, having no idea of prohibitions or of taboo, having only in mind that they were not comfortable in the hardly welcoming semi-darkness of the cabinets, but that, despite it all, their behavior responded to natural and indisputable demands, which is why, sixty years later, he remembers with no embarrassment and no shame that Eliane Schust dropped her panties in front of him and that he sniffed her behind, that Linda Woo crouched in front of him and spent a long time, thoughtfully and without commentary, examining and handling his genital organs, and that one day Jean Doïevode peed in his mouth, and he remembers that at the moment when Mourma Yogodane's questioning gaze met his, the memory of these sessions in the cabinets came to him, but that he pushed them away, conscious that in no case could he allow his imagination to waver, conscious that he mustn't at any price, even for a second, desert the narrative outpouring that he had launched into an hour earlier and of which he imagined neither interruption nor conclusion, and shortly after that the recess bell had rung, and he remembers that, while the classroom emptied, his classmates glanced at him, saying nothing and looking surprised, for one thing because he continued to write without getting up or even lifting his head, for another because Frau Mohndjee wasn't getting angry with him, wasn't making any remark, and on the contrary encouraged the students to leave without bothering him, explaining in a low voice to Jean Doïevode that he shouldn't pull on his sleeve or his hair and that he needed to remain in the room alone, away from the world, entirely alone with the story he was writing, and in this way he was able to take advantage of total solitude for a good fifteen minutes, while in the courtyard the students shouted, bickered or chased one another, played, and he remembers that he made better and faster progress and that before the end of recess he had started on a fifth notebook cover, shamelessly stolen from Jean Doïevode's stash, and that this fifth volume began with a development of insects, *And the children turned around and sawed in the sky the marshuns that wanted to clime on the bees of the forest on the wasps but they didnt manage and they killd them and the hornets arived and they surounded the marshuns and the children cried wah wah wah wah wah to make them get away and the giant buterflies was ded too,* and he remembers that at the end of recess, while the students flowed around him to take their places once again, everyone glanced at him on the sly, as though taking care not to be in contact with him, and that he thought then that he was sick, that the fever that burned in his face perhaps had another origin than the internal fire of writing, and that perhaps he had caught one of those terrifying illnesses whose existence adults often mention, and whose symptoms were unknown to him at the time, let alone the spelling, poliomyelitis, typhoid, skeletal tuberculosis, plutocratic greed, the plague.

Next to him, trailing a stinking wake of sweat and blood, stirring up the stench that their victims had emitted before dying, for the doctor and the doctor's assistant had fouled themselves when they understood that they wouldn't survive, Greta and Bruno Khatchatourian are losing patience. Once again they throw themselves on him and shove him, they hurl his wheelchair against the wall, they slap him as hard as they can. Once again they threaten to execute him if he doesn't cooperate. They haven't read any of his books, but they nonetheless haven't forgotten that he has the reputation of someone who, for ten years, has stood up to the police with weapons and explosives. His aura impresses them. He has directed commandos who carried out justice, who shot down enemies of the people while the whole world thought that egalitarian theories were as outmoded as after the Berlin Wall came down. They would like it, in the end, if he came around to their side, whether by admitting that he's been, for a thousand years, a clandestine leader of dark forces, or by tracing for them a strategy that could lead them to final victory. They don't really know, in the end, whether he's an ally to convince, or an enemy. They would like above all for him to help them to drive the dark forces out from the asylum, to prepare a list of spies, they want him to rid the world of the last nurses, of Martians, of colonialists, and of capitalism in general. They want him to make a clear decision about the capitalists that piss on the moon, about the cooks in the cafeteria, about old lady Philippe.

"I don't know," he murmurs from time to time. "I can't seem to collect my thoughts. I don't know who old lady Philippe is. I have never seen her here. Perhaps it's another story."

They rough him up, they circle around him, stepping over the bodies or sometimes stumbling on them, and they shout, they get angry, they grab his wheelchair and bash it against the cupboard, against the table, against the walls. They mutter, they scream. They torment him, but irregularly, and sometimes they once again give the impression of having forgotten that they're interrogating him. All of a sudden they start to converse or fight as if no witness were present. The dialogues have no rhyme or reason, and they're frightening.

"Old lady Philippe is on the brink of savagery," says Greta.

"That old bitch," moans Bruno Khatchatourian. "What the hell does she have to do with anything? Are you afraid she'll come down with the cannibals? Are you afraid she'll come with the pissing moon?"

"You don't get it," Greta says angrily. "Old lady Philippe is with my parents. She's going to kill them. She's going to kill everyone. She's going to kill the nurses."

"And this guy, has he been conspiring with the nurses?" asks Bruno Khatchatourian as he hits the prisoner.

"As surely as two and two are four," exclaims Greta. "He's a spy for old lady Philippe. He conspired with that bitch, with my parents, with the nurses and with the authorities."

She slaps him and she abandons him, she goes from one side to the other, stammering and kicking the bodies of the doctor and assistant. Or she heads to the window, grimaces at the outdoors, and does an about-face. Her grizzled hair flies about with her, behind her, disorderly, fluttering, flying.

She comes back towards him, towards the wheelchair.

"In any case, you're fucked," she says.

She starts to laugh cruelly. She plays with a stapler that she has picked up from the doctor's desk. She hits him in the head with it, but without trying to break his skull.

"It's not even about old lady Philippe," grumbles Bruno Khatchatourian. "This guy conspired with the Martians. He conspired with the Martians, end of story."

He punches the prisoner. He hits him in the head, in the neck.

"With the Martians and with your parents," Bruno Khatchatourian says, worked up. "We'll make him spit out the truth. He's a bastard like the others."

"He doesn't want to rid us of the Martians," says Greta. "He's been protecting them since he was a kid. He protects them like an old hen warming her brood."

"He has them in his belly and in his mind," says Bruno Khatchatourian.

"He's hatching them," shouts Greta. "He's got old lady Philippe, too! In his belly and in his mind, he's got old lady Philippe, too!"

"They've done nothing but kill us since the beginning!" shouts Bruno Khatchatourian, indignant.

They take up the beating again. They work on him for half a minute. He wavers on his seat and stays quiet.

He is lucid enough to understand that he has very little chance of making it out. The two lunatics have already amply shown that they could put anybody to death at the slightest change of mood. They have made terror reign since the morning, since they took power. Behind them, a large stream of blood, with them, a handful of furious insurgents, cannibals ready for anything, and a few murderous patients as delirious as they are. In front of them, nothing. He knows that they're not susceptible to reason and that it's better, rather, not to engage them in any discussion. Each sentence addressed to one or the other of them is received as a taunt if it doesn't coincide perfectly with their apocalyptic conception of the world. It's highly likely that suddenly, without warning, they'll drag him into the common room and lock him up with the other patients, with the hostages, in the room with all the lowered iron shutters, in the room where they've already emptied three canisters of alcohol so that they can light it on fire in case of any outside intervention. They could also very easily cut the interrogation short and kill him with a chair or shards of glass, as they did when they wasted the watchmen and the personnel. Their takeover is too far along, things have gone too far.

Their takeover is too far along.

The special psychiatric establishment is a battlefield.

Things have gone too far.

No retreat is possible.

One can just make out, in the distance, the brouhaha of police sirens, the megaphone announcements that the officers repeat as they negotiate with the group of knife-wielding schizophrenics, with the cannibals lurking near the guardhouse, and he supposes that the emergency situation specialists are now studying tactics to regain control of the site, but deep down he knows that the police won't intervene in time to save him, and that neither Greta, nor Bruno Khatchatourian, nor he will be alive when the operation is complete.

"The police," stutters Bruno Khatchatourian. "D'you hear?"

"Eh," he says.

"We hear them," says Bruno Khatchatourian. "They're getting closer."

"We're on the brink of savagery," says Greta. "We're strong. We have the situation well in hand. They won't dare to do anything to us."

"And what do we do if they put the moon before the cattle?" asks Bruno Khatchatourian.

"If old lady Philippe shakes out her apron, we set the whole thing ablaze," boasts Greta. "She is in the palm of our hand. Now she's so small. We just close our fist and she disappears."

"If they get close, we'll say that we have their leader," suggests Bruno Khatchatourian.

"They're blowing their horns," says Greta. "They're blowing the horns of the apocalypse. They don't scare us. We can also spew out the apocalypse."

"All they've gotta do is provoke us," splutters Bruno Khatchatou-rian.

"You don't get it," laments Greta, exasperated.

"They have extraterrestrials," says Bruno Khatchatourian. "We have their leader. They can't do anything to us."

"We're on the brink of savagery," Greta grimaces again. "They better not come close, the bastards."

They move more and more quickly, more and more nervously in the medical office, whose dimensions now seem cramped, for they pace every which way, and no matter what they do, they run into an obstacle. Every four or five steps they hit a wall, a piece of furniture, a body, or even their prisoner, tied to his wheelchair and trying not to see them.

He smells their odor of dirty clothes, of insane grime, of insane sweat, of blood.

The fatal moment is approaching and he has no illusions about it, but he refuses to become sad or frightened, he doesn't want to grieve uselessly at the idea of the coming execution, he doesn't want to ponder the absurdity, he refuses to deplore the death that will be inflicted on him by these fellow detainees struck by delirium and murderous rage, a situation he could have imagined in books, sure, or visualized in a romånce, but that he hadn't foreseen for himself, and he seeks to overcome his disappointment at having to die so stupidly, at the hands of former comrades or other peers, perhaps less clear than he is on the ideological map, but close, in the end, plunged into an identical unhappiness, sharing with him the exclusion, the hal-lucinations, and the solitude of madness, and refuses too to dwell on the hateful hope that he caressed a few moments earlier and that still subsists in him in traces, in the form of violent scenes at the end of which the police save him, scenes of rescue that end in embraces with the enemy, with the enemy soldiers, whose uniforms stink of military leather, frying oil, gunpowder, and blood, and it's why he delights neither in the images of his own death, nor in those of his highly unlikely deliverance, and with that eliminated, he once again pushes aside the temptation of seeing the main episodes of his failed life flash by, he doesn't want to project internally the solemn and grotesque film that will resume its course of writer and combatant, of artist-warrior having wandered endlessly in a lost war, in the territories of a war crowned by collapse and by nothingness, a radical struggle against capitalism, against the military-industrial machines, and against the intellectual buffoons of the capitalists, he doesn't wish to relive, for these extreme minutes, the lost battles, the wasted decades, the uninterrupted chain of defeats and betrayals, of arrests, of evasions, of incarcerations, life in prison, life in the camp, the terminal confinement in the system of special psychiatric establishments, and, at the same time, he wants to forget once and for all his work as a writer, so irregular and so derisory, his books, published or not, whose titles he has already forgotten, whose interconnected stories he cannot evoke except as an indistinct and graceless mass, but something resists in his consciousness, and he realizes that his mind continues to stir up a literary project that he never abandoned and that aims to regroup all of his texts, to crystalize them in a final story and even a final sentence that will put an end to the ensemble, and even a final word that will respond to the first word of the very first story, to this "begining" placed like a title on the first notebook cover, and he remembers that at the time when he was still writing, during a period when he hadn't left writing behind for the straight-jacket, he had dreamed of concluding his literary edifice, of course in a novelistic context where it would be demanded, with the word "finished" or "end," and then of withdrawing himself for good from the worries of written language, then he told himself that the project was childish, and in any case too formalistic and too pretentious, and that not having been able to write "finished" or "end" on a final page before his death is just one more defeat, a tiny, unimportant personal defeat, a microscopic defeat, and he turns his thoughts back to that October morning in Frau Mohndjee's classroom, he prefers finding himself there, at the beginning, and he sees himself again, during recess, in the empty room, feverishly molding a child's confused, inexplicable, hermetic and foundational story, and he comes back to the very first minute of his fever, and suddenly he remembers that when he got that first word down, with a brown colored pencil to which he later preferred a simple graphite pencil, he remembers that as he wrote "begining" he had the ephemeral but vertiginous sensation that he was actually continuing something and that, without managing to formulate it or understand it, he was walking along a passageway that connected him to a past life, a past existence, and he remembers that this passageway that he hadn't even really glimpsed vanished as quickly, and he also remembers the assurance with which he stripped the notebook and the workbook of their paper notebook covers, as if it were a matter of course, with an artisanal gesture that had long been a part of his daily life, even defining his daily life since the beginning of time, taking a notebook cover with the intention of tracing fictions upon it, smoothing the paper with the palm of his hand and instantly opening up a path, instantly saying in wobbly letters and wobbly words, *In a faraway country there is very mean black peeple that ar savages,* and he remembers the colors of the exercise notebook, muted crimson and muted garden green, and the illustration that was on the first page, a little boy and a little girl seen from behind, marveling at the technical progress and the comfort offered by bottled propane and butane, and he also remembers that on the back of the notebook cover there were multiplication tables, and that on the flaps appeared once again the model house, the little girl leaning over a cooking pot and the model gas tanks, and he recalls the odors of the paper, the parquet still wet with dirty water, the scent of the pencil that he clenched in his fingers, the scent of wax and the mop and his desk, but now he tries in vain to recall the images that possessed him before and during recess, he can't manage to recall the images anymore, perhaps because he's distracted by the growing rumor of the present, perhaps because the torrent of reality suddenly inflates around him and catches up to him, for on the lawn, below the medical office, he hears shouts, whistles and explosions, and while he's in the middle of telling himself that neither the workbooks, nor the notebook covers, nor his life have had any particular meaning in the world, he senses Greta and Bruno Khatchatourian running all over the room, panicked, panting, and he remembers another sentence of the text written that day, *So they sawed that the forest animals was skared and they ran away between the trees and the see and they sayed to the village children to close their eyes and they killd them and when the red poleece came out of the forest they shouted attack attack and they killd them,* and this sentence has hardly reached his memory when Greta grabs the hammer that she used to break the doctor's skull this morning, Greta brandishes the hammer and she uses it to break the windowpane and to pound on the window in the direction of the commandos who are galloping on the lawn, Greta is nothing more than a harpy in the middle of shards of glass, upturned furniture, cadavers, and the powerful stench of blood and teargas, and this harpy screams, she screams that old lady Philippe won't have the last word and that in any case it will end, and he feels a wave of satisfaction pass over him, he thinks that his life has obeyed, despite everything, a certain logic, that the loop is closing basically well, despite circumstances to the contrary, and Greta approaches him, she brings her hammer down on his clavicles, on his skull, and she kills him, and with an inhuman voice of murderous rage, again and again she screams it will end it will end it will end.

Ah, he thinks. And she, once again, she screams: It will end.

WITHOUT MARTA AND Boris Bielouguine, who plucked me from the swamp that I had unhappily fallen into along with the bag containing my manuscript, I never would have been able to carry out my literary enterprise and give the final version of *A Meeting at the Boyols'* to my editor. So here I insist on warmly thanking Marta and Boris, two exquisite people who knew, with great presence of mind, to go and find the salvific ropes and boards, as well as the blanket with a lovely Scottish pattern under which I was able to regain my spirits.

I also won't forget, this goes without saying, Ravial and Edma Mawashee, whose precious advice helped me as I prepared my journey into Amazonia, and their friend Dolmar Dong, who generously hosted me in his hacienda when, my plane having been rerouted, I landed in Buenos Aires.

Thanks also go to Miliya Forbane, who, during the going-away party, allowed me to touch and kiss her delicious breasts, which inspired the end of *Mlatelpopec in Paradise.*

Grad Litrif and his companion Lioudmila introduced me to the head of the Marbachvili archives, and thanks to their intervention I was able to access the notebooks of Vulcain Marbachvili, from which I was able, for my story *Long Ago to Bed Early,* to copy several sentences before the earthquake struck that engulfed the archives. My thanks to these three people, and apologies to the archivist, as I was sadly unable to locate either her name or her body in the rubble.

My novel *Going-Away Party* owes a tremendous amount to the following people, whom I thank with all my heart: Oliouda Alayomian, Dream Lee-Ouravienko, Dream Lifchitz, Biela Kamaleya, Meehi Dadjanal, Lola Gavrakis, Tiryane Balafron, Idiyine Taramezian, Irina Gam, Irina Nirvanian, Kirioucha Galbar, Dodnaya Drandz, Meema Kronstadt, Solonia Karakassian. Without their help, sometimes perfunctory and limited, sometimes, on the contrary, substantial, I could not have completed my writing project. May they all know that my gratitude towards them is great and forever inalterable.

Thank you to Grigoria Balsamian who was the first to suggest that I recount the adventure of Mica Schmitz and her tragic exploration of Lac Bleu, an adventure which prior to my choosing it as the central theme of *Sun of the Just* hadn't elicited any novelistic echo and remained totally unknown to the public and even to the authorities charged with protecting the lake. Thank you to Julius Ritchmann, father of Grigoria, who made the postcard from Mica Schmitz available to me, on the basis of which I was able to begin my investigation. Thank you to Bernardo Balsamian, husband of Grigoria, for having transported me several times from the train station to his country house, and for the discretion with which he distanced himself from the villa during the long afternoons when I exchanged with Grigoria the intimate words that would later enrich the first pages of *Sun of the Just*. Thank you, finally, to Grigoria Balsamian's gardener, Halfar Sharanogar, who one day had the presence of mind to detain Bernardo Balsamian in the orchard while Grigoria and I showered and got dressed again.

Thanks to Sheeva Drahane, who, during the going-away party and at a moment when I least expected it, disrobed before me, and had the kindness to encourage me to do the same before showing me the way to room 801 and penetrating it in my company. The sixth chapter of *Tomorrow the Otters* could not have been written without the sweetness of this encounter.

These acknowledgements would be particularly incomplete if I didn't include Myriam Wundersee, whose great political erudition and whose contacts in the world of subversion in northern Europe allowed me to evoke, without too many errors, the "White Fang" networks, as well as the "Valpolicella" network and the militants of the radical left of Iceland. If, by chance, any incongruities have slipped into my descriptions, the fault cannot be attributed to her, and only my authorial imprudence is responsible. To the precious information that Myriam Wundersee provided me without the slightest reticence, I'd like to add here, as they also merit warm and eternal thanks, Myriam Wundersee's grace, her laugh, her availability at all moments, as well as her unsurpassed *osso buco alla romana*.

Among the people to whom I am deeply indebted for having sustained me in difficult moments, a very special place must be reserved for

Tatiana Vidal, to her husband Olaf, and even to their baby Carmelita for the encouragement that they provided me when, intending to throw myself out the window, I had already stepped over the edge of their twenty-second floor balcony. Without their comforting, intelligent, and appropriate words, and without the strident sobs of Carmelita, I fully believe that I never would have finished my novel *Macbeth in Paradise.*

Thanks to Roger Chabert for explaining the rules of Sudoku and Go to me, which my characters Timothy Kerrygan and Franko Salieri used to their advantage in my novella *Voices of Skulls.*

My novel *Eve of Pandemic* would not have had such medical verisimilitude if Madame Patricia Mourabenne, called Patou, hadn't shown me, with an abnegation that honors her, the scars that mark the base of her shoulder, the hollow of her groin, and around her ankles. May she be warmly thanked here.

The collection of stuffed guinea pigs that so intrigues my detective Julien Gardel at the beginning of the novel *The Old Women Walking By* was lent to me in a way by Monsieur and Madame Alchaïa from Casablanca. I don't know how to thank them enough for allowing me to enter the room where their personal collection is piously stored, for permitting me to take a photograph, and for thinking to recount to me in detail the existence and the personality of each of their eighty-eight guinea pigs.

While I was doing research at the central library of São Paulo for my novel *Shipwreck on the Curuguri*, a heavy book fell from a high shelf where it had been relegated with other doctoral monstrosities of its sort, and flying in front of my face, it grazed my forehead. I will not express any thanks to its author, who devoted several years to plundering Tupu-Guarani dictionaries in order to take inventory and comment on *The Names of Vegetables and Tubers in Contemporary Brazilian Literature.* By contrast, I will mention Venus Vieira, the young publishing intern who put pressure on my wound while I, astonished by the abundance of my blood and by the inanity of certain university works, flipped through a one hundred and sixty-page chapter dedicated to black beans in writings from between the two world wars. First aid complete, Venus Vieira invited me to her home so that she could closely monitor the evolution of my scar. I will never forget the several nights that I spent with her, nor the cinnamon scent of her hair, nor the extremely calming audacity of her caresses on my forehead and elsewhere.

Without establishing a hierarchy of their merit, I will here warmly thank the co-detainees with whom I shared the forty weeks of my incarceration in Yogyakarta, and, in particular, the leader of the Muslim Bang cell, who forbid the prisoners on the floor from sodomizing me and who taught me the subtleties of the use of timers planted in a bar of plastic, subtleties that are developed in *Goodbye Clouds*.

A vibrant thank-you to the person who gave me his seat in the Prospekt Shaumyana-Nevsky Prospekt tramway in Leningrad, which allowed me to take dictation of the words of the song "Maple," hummed next to me by Maria Lobanova, whom I also thank here for her numerous indications on the Russian lyric song, for her transcription of several impossible-to-find poems by Yesenin, and also, of course, for the two marvelous nights that I spent in her company at the Ladoga Hotel.

Also present among the people who helped me to turn the corner when I was struggling to finish *Hell in Paradise*, I will never know how to sufficiently express my thanks to the Boppe brothers, whose music combining their Slavic roots and the songs of Louisiana often comforted me, alternating of course with the nine symphonies of Gustav Mahler, a musician whom I thank posthumously with all my heart and with all my ears.

These acknowledgments would lose a large part of their worth if they neglected Rita Botticelli, who during the going-away party took the initiative of leading me to a dim and deserted boudoir, in order to do with me the things that I describe in the ninth chapter of *Smoke at Dusk*, then, while her husband and his three bodyguards tried to figure out where she had disappeared to, hid with me in the closet, where we continued to do those things.

It is especially agreeable to me to extend my thanks to Pranda Toumararana, who not only helped me to mount Sultan Labibi's personal elephant, but also, seeing that we were headed towards an impasse, helped me to get back down. This episode can be found, almost exactly as it happened, in *Goodbye, Romeo*. Without Pranda Toumararana, it would obviously have finished very badly.

I deplore that the authorities haven't implemented my proposition to reintroduce threatening species in urban zones including, notably, anthropophagi, ear-cutters, Pol Pot supporters, and headshrinkers. This reintroduction would assure a greater biodiversity in large cities and I was counting on it to give a more realistic terrain to my novels *Square One* and *An Endless Tunnel*. I thank the pensioners in the psychiatric clinic who were confined with me for two years in the same dormitory and who, sharing my views, did not cede under pressure and affixed their six names to the bottom of the petition that demanded this measure, at the same time as our unconditional liberation.

Thanks to the helping hands of Irigaël Bugbol, Dama Bugbol, Sachka Bugbol, Anderia Bugbol, and little Abimaël Bugbol, I was able to clear the rubble that, after the explosion of the neighboring factory, had buried Natalia Bugbol as well as the materials necessary for editing *Bogus Five* and the draft of *Journal of Pandemonium*. Without their objective assistance, I wouldn't have had the courage to rework these two books. Natalia Bugbol is, it goes without saying, included in these thanks, even if her state did not permit her to participate in the clearing.

Diodora and Banzer Malfinghal opened their doors to me during the famous meteor shower that, in Jelgava, Latvia, was quite rightly considered to be the initial phase of the apocalypse. I was a complete stranger to them in that moment and I see in their gesture the proof that human beings in large cities can remain honorable, despite adverse circumstances and cataclysmic events. Thanks to this generously opened door, I was able to continue my existence from the very next day in what remained of Jelgava, and later to write the end of the second part of *The Blue Hougane*. May Diodora and Banzer know that I haven't forgotten them, either of them, even if, following the fire in the city and the panic that followed, I lost them forever.

Thanks to my sister Birgit, who put up with me without recrimination during the editing of *Metamorphosis of the Assassin*, and to her husband Roberto, who didn't put up with me, but who had the patience the next year to reread the proofs of this sizable volume, and whose judicious recommendations regarding apparently insoluble problems of agreement I had the pleasure of following.

It would seem unfair not to mention prominently among those to whom I wish to express my gratitude, my sister Birgit's dog Ramses, who, several times, alerted me to the approach of unwelcome visitors, and with a rare intelligence, kept them at bay, until I was able to hide in the guest room and play dead.

Thanks also to Laïla Dromschel, to Marion Terbenian, and to Djeena Murmaduk, who during the going-away party, under the influence of alcohol or for some other reason, collectively promised to let me taste the delights of their admirable bodies, a promise that was not kept but that remains inscribed in me always, and the fact that it was pronounced touches me deeply.

In its scenes of torrential rain, my novel *Flood* would have had no likeness to reality if I hadn't listened carefully to the explanations of Madame Morgenplatt, meteorologist for the Belgian consulate in Hong Kong, who scrupulously corrected all my approximations on typhoons and, after the buffet dinner offered by the consul, allowed me to access all the secret documentation of the consulate, and of Belgium in general, concerning tropical storms and depressions in Southeast Asia.

I do not intend to leave Petit Petia in the shadows, son of my former peers in the services, now retired from all activity and leading a completely normal life under the identities of Macha and Stefan. Petit Petia started to speak when I embarked on the first chapter of *Faces in the Factory*. The conversations with Petit Petia and with his numerous four-legged friends helped me considerably in forging the character of Doublon, the little boy who the killers in *Faces in the Factory* never manage to catch. Naturally my wish for Petit Petia is that he, too, may escape killers, if ever the latter, in retaliation for forgotten misdeeds of his parents, get the idea to launch a pursuit.

Thanks to the archivist at the synagogue in Prague, A.T., who, after having searched with me in vain for Franz Kafka's date of birth, invited me to the corner tavern for an impromptu dinner, and perhaps would have permitted me to accompany her back to her apartment, which wasn't very far away, if her boyfriend hadn't burst into the tavern and clearly demonstrated his intention of taking care of that affair himself.

Thanks to my then editor, Malcom Okada, who suggested that I title my first novel *To the Reunited Flesh*, when I was planning on using the title *Essay on Duality*.

While I was lost in the labyrinthine discourse that wasn't at all helping my detective Horacio Hirsch find his way back to heart of the action, the owner of the café on Rue des Savetiers-Héroïques, who saw that I was attempting to cross a difficult pass, automatically served me a fifth mulled wine. It was after having drunk this comforting brew that I decided to cancel all the parasitic chatter of the thirteenth chapter of *Morituri* and to kill Horacio Hirsch, which imparted a much greater readability to the work. The owner of the café on Rue des Savetiers-Héroïques being distinctly associated with this essential dramatic turn, I simply must mention him among the people to whom I am grateful.

Another person to whom I owe my eternal, or, at any rate, lasting gratitude is Madame Tarachenko, with whom I often spoke on the phone when I was quarantined in Bishkek, in the hospital located just across from the maternity ward where she was medical secretary, and who was my only true interlocutor at Bishkek during those three long weeks of forced isolation. The content of our conversations is partially reproduced in my novella *Chaos in Kyrgyzstan*, as well as the description of the lamb kebabs that she obligingly had delivered several times to my room, potential plague victim that I was.

It is time to thank with greatest fervor and emotion Yleenia Yam and Mimna Agaldibuk, without whom I would never have managed to get out of the attic where I had been locked up by their cousins, who were also their pimps. Without their decisive intervention, I think I can say that my subsequent publications would have been posthumous without exception. I will also remember until my death the mole that one of them had on her left buttock, while nonetheless regretting that I no longer know if the buttock belonged to Yleenia Yam or to Mimna Agaldibuk.

My heartfelt thanks also go to Marta Goldanska, who, while I was writing *"Titanic" to Port*, lived under another identity and never called herself either Marta or Goldanska. She would have hated to be publicly cited, but I am certain that, if she reads these lines, she will recognize herself.

The baggage handlers at the airport in Managua who lost my three suitcases of manuscripts, as well as the mysterious woman traveling on the Managua-Tegucigalpa flight who inherited them and who abstained from restoring them to me, thereby depriving me of the profit of five years of work, deserve to be mentioned here, but one will understand that they must not wait for my thanks.

I do not thank Abel Daradanski, Donald Bocks, Roum Marchadian, Oleg Strelnikov, Chico Rausch, Anabela Janvier, Ilda Lorca, Gamal Tretiakov, Simon Tatha, Jak Ferricali, Urban Zawaliewski, Henri Loubier, Fernanda Saori, Mina Legallin, Maroussia Begueyan, Wilfried Ribero, Norman Hedrad, Hubert Plissonnier, Laurent Houdin, Jean-Claude Cameron, whose malicious critiques, mean-spirited little reviews, and unpardonable silences carried substantial weight towards my books' lack of success and my own relegation to the heart of the guild of difficult authors, to which I do not belong and towards which I have no sympathy.

All my thanks, in contrast, to Liza Pavarotti, who introduced me to the depths of Valparaiso, and knew how to extract me when things went awry. Thanks to her, I escaped three beatings in sailors' dive bars, as well as the eighteen knife-slashes that the captain of the container ship *Rigoletto* promised me, and that finally peppered my ephemeral drinking companion Ram Aquilino. To Liza Pavarotti I send a nostalgic salute, for she has more than a little to do with the apparition of the luminous, nameless prostitute in my novel *School of Bandits*. As for the widow of Ram Aquilino, I can say nothing here that will alleviate her chagrin, though she has secured my most sorrowful sentiments.

Liena Babenko kept an eye on my toiletries and my address book during my expedition into Chernobyl's forbidden zone. After a restorative shower taken at Liena Babenko's home, I was pleased to find my aftershave, as well as clean sheets between which she slipped right away, with great appropriateness and without reproaching me at all for my radioactivity. For this caretaking, and for this embrace that I hardly expected, Liena Babenko remains in my memory as an example of generosity and disinterested Ukrainian tenderness.

I would feel horribly ungrateful if I did not take advantage of this opportunity to affectionately praise the work of the "Happy Days" theater troupe, which had the courage to add my unique play, *Djann's Awakening*, to its repertoire, and, having performed it two evenings in a row before a rigorously empty room, nevertheless held to performing a third showing the following Saturday, taking clear pleasure in it, and not ascribing any importance to the obvious absence of spectators yet again.

Nothing would have been the same in my books that feature the non-sighted if I hadn't had the support of the powerful Association for the Blind of Northern Canada, which made available to me its braille works on the little-known techniques of long-distance communication during snowstorms. Furthermore, I wouldn't have been able to decipher these works without the dexterous fingers of the librarian Nounrane Lonsdale, who allowed me to call her Noune and who translated the braille with stupefying speed. The gentle voice of Nounrane Lonsdale, unforgettable, still resonates as soon as I evoke those studious hours. I didn't use the information that I gleaned and I regret having thus abandoned, in the midst of the howling storm and with no means of calling for help, my heroine Maria Bachmann, but in the same book, *Storm Over Madeleine Polpot*, Nounrane Lonsdale is easily recognizable in the young blind woman who soliloquizes before a village idiot.

Thanks to my friend Fredo Chang, who uncovered for me the permanent address of the mad Arab Abdul Alhazred, author of *Necronomicon*, and who firmly incited me to go on location to verify that the book really existed and that its famous author had neither died in 743 in Damascus, nor was he insane, nor a legend. Out of cowardice, I did not hurry to reach number 9, rue de la Montagne-au-Chaudron in Brussels, where the poet occupied a rather vast apartment, according to Fredo Chang. On the other hand I did take notes on this luxurious residence, which had nothing Lovecraftian about it, and I described it in my novel *New Life*.

During the going-away party, the beautiful Emilia Togliatta responded to my advances and we were able, for three-quarters of an hour, to isolate ourselves in a bathroom on the eighth floor and fornicate marvelously there. For what happened during this time of isolation, for Emilia Togliatta's hair flying around me in all directions, for her inventive frenzy and her abandon, and also for the words that she spoke as we went back down to the floor where the reception was taking place, I remain eternally grateful to this exceptional woman. The declaration of love that she whispered in my ear in the elevator was reproduced, albeit in a willingly less personal manner, at the end of *Gleams in the Hold*.

I won't leave in the shadows the acrobats of the Zapata circus, with whom I found myself on an excursion to an Incan site, and whose intervention was decisive at the moment when I worked on my novel *Malone in Paradise*, more precisely at a moment when I had rather foolishly wanted to test the aptitudes of my character Mordechaï Malone to battle vertigo and found myself suspended, numb with fear, between Huayna Picchu and Machu Picchu, fifteen feet below the nearest trail. The acrobats formed a human chain and saved Mordechaï Malone, myself, and the forthcoming book all at once.

A heartfelt thank-you to Rada Petigros, Miliya Santanden, Vicky Müller, Anastasia Loukovaïa, Raïa Ourdouk. They know why.

It is not customary to thank tigers. I nevertheless give thanks to the pair of tigresses at the Singapore zoo, two splendid animals into whose home I made a nocturnal incursion after a very, very boozy party, accompanied by a certain Mario Bumaputrak, who claimed he could hold his whisky better than I my mai tai. Once inside the enclosure, and when we had nothing left to drink, my companion started to pick a fight with me. The male grunted in its cage but did not come out, unlike the two females who seemed interested in our drunken quarrel. I thank these two powerful creatures for having immediately taken my side by tearing Mario Bumaputrak to pieces, and furthermore for having judged my extremely mai tai-charged breath to be repulsive. They shared Mario Bumaputrak and they let me retreat across the enclosure and then slowly scale the barbed grate that separated the pit from the rest of the world. For this benevolence on my behalf, it seems necessary to mention them here.

I will obviously not thank the TV host Omer Faraone. He knows why.

Thanks to Madame Wassila Saarfadine, caretaker at the mysterious bird cemetery in Boufarik, not only because she guided me between the tombs when I had lost my way, but also because she tried to imitate for me the discordant song of the bald ibis, which dissuaded me from introducing this birdsong into the last part of *Loose Shells*, despite the fact that ibis play more than a passing role in it.

I feel indisputably and immensely indebted to my non-sighted friends Irina and Viktor Darbakcheïev, who, during the Vologda massacre, of which I tried to give an account in my book *Last Shooting Before the Grave*, spent hours passing me the requisite cartridges and clips, being unable, for obvious reasons, to take a more direct role in the shoot-out.

For nineteen years I kept up an amorous correspondence with the deeply mourned Nadienka Kim. Thanks to her spouse Kim Byung-chun for having offered to return to me the two suitcases that contained all my letters. The suitcases were destroyed in transit and I think that destiny was wise in proceeding in this way. I would have had a terrible conscience, in fact, of recopying them in my epistolary novel *A Future Widow*, and, furthermore, I would have hated to leave them in an attic, lamentably exposed to degradation, dust, and oblivion.

While this list, so agreeable to create, must end despite it all, I regret that several thousands of people are not included in it, of which my readers are obviously a part, who to one degree or another, by their anonymous presence, were associated with this or that novelistic episode, or helped me not to lose confidence, or individually or collectively modified my perception of things. From this almost numberless crowd, for, to the thousands of the living, I would add the millions of the dead, I would like to extract, as standard-bearer for all, and to receive in their name my great thanks to them, Guerassim Prokofiev, whose death notice I copy here as it can be found in the lists of executions of the Butovo Polygon: Prokofiev Guerassim Ivanovich, born in 1880, Moscow region, Zagorsk district, village of Golyguino; Russian; elementary education; no party; nursing aide at municipal hospital No. 2. Address: Moscow, Kalujskaya Ulitsa, 22, building 5, apartment 45. Arrested March 1, 1938. Judgment pronounced by a troika of regional OUNKVD on June 3, 1938. Charge: in December 1937 destroyed a brochure that was entrusted to him, *Regulatory Texts for Elections to the Supreme Soviet of the USSR*, and expressed his discontent with regard to the augmentation of the length of the workday. Shot on June 27, 1938. Buried in Butovo, Moscow region.

THE STRATEGY OF SILENCE IN THE WORK OF BOGDAN TARASSIEV

No INITIATIVE MARKED the fiftieth anniversary of the death of Bogdan Tarassiev, also known—if the term "known" means anything, with regard to a writer—by the pseudonym Jean Balbaïan.

Here we will evoke this singular author's path, and we will lean especially on a particularity of his work, which, it would seem, has had no equal to this day. It concerns a process whose manifestation is a lack of variety in the names given to characters. Firmly established and clearly differentiated at the level of the plot, heroes and even secondary figures are cloaked in identities so phonetically close that the reader tends to confuse them. In the texts that we will examine in a moment, for example, Tarassiev names all of the shades that he portrays, whether living or dead, Woolf, Walef, Woluf, Wlaff, and Folf; in his last text, only the name Wolff is used.

Such a standardization of character names does not signal a mere artistic whim. It must be analyzed as a decisive literary orientation, and, if we consider it in conjunction with what we know of the life of Tarassiev, it must also be understood as a gesture of adhesion to the most radical philosophies of nothingness as well.

Bogdan Tarassiev started his career as an author in 2017, under the name of Jean Balbaïan, by publishing a crime novel series.

His detectives work in indeterminate cosmopolitan cities, akin to post-atomic urban concentrations, set against backdrops of surveillance-free camps and steppes open to the four winds, like a traveler before the war could still roam in Tibet or on the Mongolian plateau. Although it doesn't align with the artificial complexity of the literary avant-garde, Tarassiev's manner of writing breaks with the style and even the tradition of popular realism. We remain within the category of crime novels, and a criminal investigation occupies a central spot in the story, but the framing is unusual. The context is always political chaos and nighttime; the characters speak little; rather than progressing through a universe familiar to the reader, they plunge into troubled underworlds, they carry out obscure rituals; the world in which the action takes place is rooted in a society closed in on itself, totalitarian, that functions on intellectual barbarity, propaganda, and lies. Detectives, victims, and assassins get lost within, and aside from the rare enthusiasts of post-exoticism, readers balk at wandering along with them all the way to the last page.

For a crime novel reader to absorb the text and take pleasure in reading it, it is of course necessary that he or she be able to establish links of familiarity between his or her personal universe and the book's universe. The detective must lead a clear investigation, with the goal being the triumph of justice or, at least, of the truth, and the actors must evolve according to codes with legible moral values. The reader must be able to translate what he or she reads by bringing to it his or her own experience, the one that has crystalized through leading his or her life or in reading other books. These conditions are neglected in Tarassiev's narrative device. The reader has the impression of accompanying unlikeable characters within a suffocating, troubling, opaque adventure, of which he or she senses the echoes and the fears without really being invited to become a part of it.

Retrospectively, today, one can evaluate these texts as being exceptionally original. Bogdan Tarassiev constructed a parallel world and explored it by bringing forth captivating images, capable of haunting the reader for a long time. But to be completely honest, one must admit that the plot lines of these books, while all respecting the schemas of mystery novels, didn't have the breathless nature that readers passionate about the collection were expecting: the detective aspect of the story was too often countered by the surrealist effects of shadows and stagnation.

In short, these five books under Jean Balbaïan's name did not appeal to the public. As for reviewers, they rarely expressed their thoughts on Balbaïan, but when they did, they were scathing. According to them, Balbaïan had no place among crime novelists, much less elsewhere. Balbaïan was a writer who hadn't mastered the rules of suspense, his stories had neither head nor tail, his heroes were implausible, and, behind a supposed literary non-conformism, he badly masked his inability to create a sense of atmosphere, to describe an environment, and to paint the characters.

The editor liked Balbaïan's work, but this negative reception, accompanied by sales figures much below average for the collection, dissuaded him from taking the sixth manuscript that Tarassiev proposed. Chagrined, Tarassiev retrieved the original and destroyed it. He didn't burn it with theatrical flair, before tearful witnesses; he threw it in the trash without even looking to see what vegetable peelings broke its fall. He did the same with the drafts and the two floppy disks that could have enabled him to make the book come back to life.

It was 2021. After four years of editorial activity and five out-of-the-ordinary novels, Jean Balbaïan had decided to disappear.

Here are the titles of works written by Bogdan Tarassiev under the pseudonym of Jean Balbaïan: *Encounter with the Infanta; A Shepherd of Souls; Mayayo Calls Robert Mayayo; Tamdjir's Maidservants; All the Venoms of the World.*

Assuming that it ever left a trace, the memory of Jean Balbaïan vanished rapidly. In the publishing world, it was as though he had never existed. None of the five titles were reprinted in 2025 when Black Thumb, the publisher that held the rights, was sold to a larger publishing house—not even *Tamdjir's Maidservants*, which remains, by all accounts, the most beautiful work in the Black Thumb catalog.

Bogdan Tarassiev had endured the publication experience passively; he had endured it without joy and didn't seek to repeat it, for it had, above all, brought him annoyances, disappointments and humiliations. He preferred silence, he had chosen to keep quiet. He kept quiet for twenty-three years.

We have too great a tendency to imagine that book releases modify the social standing of those whose names are on the cover. We fantasize about the idea of success, we see gold and opulence behind the piles of books. We envy the writer his sudden fortune. In reality, absolutely nothing happens on the social level, and excepting the exceptional cases, the sums paid by the publisher are simply insulting. In the case of Tarassiev-Balbaïan, what he had earned with his five books didn't equal, shall we say, what an apartment porter could collect in two weeks' worth of gratuities. The balance sheet of the supposedly prestigious activity came down to just that, a paltry handful of dollars; add to that a few disastrous press clippings and the fact that from then on most of his friends, out of embarrassment or jealousy, had broken away from him or given him the cold shoulder.

Bogdan Tarassiev had been trained as an accountant and that, despite an economic crisis already in full swing, guaranteed him stable employment. He had been hired in 2019 by an international aid organization for the poor, where he had first worked as a volunteer. He existed there for a quarter of a century, in a comfortless office, watching, in the guise of numbers, the international crimes of those who govern and the movements of generosity that the crimes generate among the governed.

One might imagine that he also composed several texts, but we have no concrete indication of his writerly activity during this long period. Out of humility, but also because the occasion never presented itself, because nobody asked him in time about his writing style or about what he hoped to communicate through his books, Bogdan Tarassiev has recounted nowhere what this interminable silence in his life as a writer signified, practically and theoretically, relative to his creative acts, to his imagination.

Provided that it can be confirmed, it seems that neither Will Pilgrimm, his former editor, nor any readers, nor anyone who might have been close to him, put any pressure on Tarassiev to take up writing again, to produce new books, to prolong the building-up of his novelistic universe. It's hard to believe that such a mark of disinterest could be inflicted upon such an author, but there you have it. These things happen.

After this period of complete silence, Tarassiev nonetheless comes back on the literary scene. He no longer hides behind a pseudonym, he doesn't state anywhere that he has already published five books, he doesn't lay claim to Jean Balbaïan's portfolio, and it's under his true patronymic, Bogdan Tarassiev—a name perfectly unknown in the republic of letters—that in the year 2044 he presents a new work, *Street of Beggar Women*.

The manuscript circulated among several publishers before being accepted, barely, by Lambda Press, directed at the time by Franck Markovic. *Street of Beggar Women* was taken on with reluctance, for its subject was shocking, but an internal report from the reading committee praises "the original voice that expresses itself without ever yielding on a stylistic level" and esteems that "its extraordinary violence will certainly create shock in the media and generate commercial appeal."

Comparing *Street of Beggar Women* to other books with approximately the same release date gives the clear sense that we're looking at a high-caliber text, a particularly successful literary object, but at the same time, we realize that it creates a stain on the landscape. Tarassiev's novel describes a social cataclysm, the absolute impoverishment of an entire region of the globe. Its characters are psychologically unstable men and women who kill one another to gain access to a rations distribution network controlled by the army and the mafia. The period, the cities, the institutions, the languages in which the heroes express themselves are imaginary, but baked from the same dough that contains all the elements of the contemporary occidental world.

The depiction of a future made of devastation and misery is not, in itself, a new literary enterprise. Science-fiction writers have treated the subject in depth, substituting social anguish due to economic crisis, or due to the politico-warmonger or mafiaesque wanderings of our governments, in works that are sometimes as powerful as the great social literature classics, and richer in unforgettable images.

Street of Beggar Women, however, is not organized like science-fiction novels, and unlike the latter, it doesn't abound in metaphors offered up to the reader for easy decryption. Equivalences and analogies do exist in *Street of Beggar Women*, but are more often coincidences than intentional connections, and the narrative world refers to nothing but itself. It is closed, constructed with a familiar reality so distorted that it is no longer transposable. It must be recognized as such rather than seeing in it a shifted description of our own.

Furthermore, the promenade in *Street of Beggar Women* is of a blackness incommensurate with the amusement that science-fiction literature typically offers, not so much because the décor is dark, but because it is obsessively traversed by fear, by intense intimate disgust, and especially by the moral obliteration of Wolff, the narrator. The overwhelmed voice of the narrator occupies the forefront of the book, imposing itself over everything, over the course of events, it's an obligatory filter to gaining an understanding of the story. Yet, from one end of *Street of Beggar Women* to the other, the reader moves through the interior of a gory and muddy misery that is absolutely intolerable to the narrator. The reader is dragged through it at the same time as Wolff and he can neither escape from the muck nor distance himself from Wolff's discourse, with his memory, his ruminations, and also his blocks and silences. One could analyze the phenomenon by saying that Wolff's voice functions like a trap: entry is immediate and easy, but escape—by which we mean a give-and-take between the discomfort of the fictional world and the comfort of the reader—is not possible in the course of reading. Wolff's world reduces itself to a horrible journey. The reading of *Street of Beggar Women* is hypnotizing, but it's also a horrible journey.

Street of Beggar Women bears no relationship to the traditions or the narrative conventions of works edited in the 40s of the 21st century. Relying more on this glaring difference than on the book's theme, Franck Markovic calculates that the novel will be noticed and the sales figures will be reasonable.

But Lambda Press's commercial projections prove futile. Though the publishing house benefits from a favorable impression in literary circles, and though a bona fide media network regularly supports the titles from its catalog, journalists are put off by *Street of Beggar Women*. They don't devote a single laudatory or disapproving article to it, they mention its existence nowhere. A dismaying silence greets Tarassiev's reappearance in the publishing arena.

This all-too-discreet renaissance nonetheless provokes no bitterness in Tarassiev. It suits the author, who in the course of his twenty-three years of mute retreat has spent enough time meditating to understand that he can expect nothing from publication. It suits his particular literary strategies, which now consist of evacuating all hope of notoriety and, on the contrary, finding a way for his texts to survive in the least flashy way possible, in scorning the hostile environment that surrounds them and in dreaming of hypothetical readers, located in the future and in the beyond. At this stage in his literary journey, it's as though he has developed a poetics for his own personal use—according to which the execrable reception of his books becomes a necessary condition for quality and existence.

And yet, in 2044 Bogdan Tarassiev's desire to be published is obvious. Without waiting for the release of *Street of Beggar Women*, thus still at a moment when his editor hopes for appreciable results for the novel, Tarassiev proposes a thick volume to Lambda Press called *Return to the Murderhouse*. After a six-week-long review, Franck Markovic asks Tarassiev to rework his manuscript, on the pretext that it is too ambitious and could be cleaved into two distinct novels.

Lambda Press's response arrives right as *Street of Beggar Women* has been distributed to bookstores and once it is already clear that the book will not be successful. The editor lost his bet, which influences his relationship with Tarassiev. One might think that from then on Lambda Press would feel nothing but indifference towards Tarassiev's work, and that Markovic, who nonetheless defended it, discovers what Tarassiev really is: a worn-out, middle-aged man, useless for the press and lacking any readers.

Tarassiev reworks his manuscript with exceptional speed—one month—which suggests, not without cynicism, that he had prepared the entire affair in advance. He cleaves *Return to the Murderhouse* into two small novels: *Ransacked* and *Fatal Alliance*. He introduces judicious breaths, he lightens it up where required, and above all, he modifies the characters' names. In his initial manuscript, the male protagonists were called Tanaz Bielgorian, Prichvine, Tim, Golovienko, Ishtvan Cranach. In the two novels that replace this version, the same five characters are named Walef, Wlaff, and Wolff. This last patronymic (which appeared on every page, as already noted, in *Street of Beggar Women*) is attributed to Golovienko, the primary narrator in *Ransacked*, and to Tim, the romantic companion of the main heroine in *Fatal Alliance*.

Suddenly, we have three novels carried more or less on the words of a certain Wolff. In *Street of Beggar Women*, Wolff is a sort of tall and ageless burn victim; in *Ransacked*, he's a street kid; and finally, in *Fatal Alliance*, Wolff is a fugitive spy, the brother of Millie Flanders, with whom he maintains an incestuous relationship. In all of these books, Wolff shoulders personalities that have nothing in common with one another, and whose voices sound radically different, even if, in the course of the three narratives, they see similar discourses rise up around them, monologues that arise from the depths of the crowds, when they don't emerge from the intimate depths of Bogdan Tarassiev himself.

Out of inertia, perhaps, or because the decision to refuse all of Tarassiev's works has not yet been made, or because the insignificant sales of *Street of Beggar Women* permit them not to pay the author an advance, Lambda Press signs a contract for *Ransacked* and *Fatal Alliance*. Nobody advised Tarassiev to modify the names of his narrators, and if anyone suggested it, they must have later come around to the logical counterargument that the author would undoubtedly defend: *Street of Beggar Women* having had practically no public existence, there was no downside to re-appropriating the name of its main character for two other stories. It's also possible that the members of the reading committee didn't read the two new manuscripts with as much attention as might be desired.

Bogdan Tarassiev's two novels appear one year apart, in 2045 and 2046, in a context that, objectively, could be to their advantage: no book of any merit appeared on the market at the same time as them. No original voice competes with them. And yet, the press reviews are rare and disappointing. The subjects that Tarassiev addresses hold not even the faintest appeal for the critics, and although they haven't opened the books, they preemptively condemn both the form and the content. They visibly have no desire to welcome Tarassiev among the writers that may one day be worthy of their praises. They are content to signal the title in the list of new releases without accompanying it with the least personal observation. Tarassiev's style, his practice of anthroponymy, and his systems of images displease them, but they can't even be bothered to say it. These embryos of commentary are not sufficient to make the books known, they reach few readers, they leave bookstores indifferent. Nonetheless, a small miracle occurs: in the circle of cursed poets and young journal editors, Tarassiev acquires a quiet reputation as an author to watch.

This is a period when, suffering from psoriatic arthritis and respiratory problems, Tarassiev requests to work part-time, then to retire.

He quickly finds himself incredibly isolated. One might think that this doesn't bother him, and that he has always shared with his characters the taste for marginalization and exile. He hardly keeps up any relationship with Lambda Press and, more generally, with the handful of living beings who might be susceptible to exchanging a friendly sentence or two with him. He does not appear anywhere in public.

He devotes this time of monastic enclosure to two activities: first of all, he writes his masterpiece, *Wolff*; and second, he writes texts for journals that have solicited them from him. His name, in fact, has begun to circulate among the editorial boards of very small publications, ephemeral journals with small print runs, not always non-conformist, but always sympathetic. Let us cite, among others, *Waxes, The Female of the Hydropath, Scarlet Babel, Ink Monkeys.* He sometimes receives requests for collaborations, and he responds in the affirmative.

The delays between submission and publication of his texts are long and uneven, and hence something happens that Tarassiev may have subconsciously desired, which may also be the result of a risky calculation, or of a deft maneuver on his part: all the prose pieces that he has sent to various journals appear at the same time, in autumn 2048, within a very short interval.

They're mainly dense stories, not always short, irreproachable in terms of their writing, that take place in the universes of Tarassiev's own creation, always somber and tattered, traversed by extraordinary images and hallucinations. The plot lines don't overlap, the players are very clearly distinct, but the names of the characters are impossible to remember once one begins to read several stories in a row. The names of the protagonists are so close that they are easily confused: Wolff, of course, which he has named a central character four times in a row, but also Woolf, Wolfo, Wulf, Walef, Woluf, Wollof, Wulw, Hollph, Hulluf, Wulluff, Wloffo, Wlaf, Walfo, Wolwö, Folf, Flöff, Wulwö, Wulwo, and Wolup.

This phenomenon is so remarkable that it eventually catches the eye of one of the canonical writers with greatest visibility in the 40s, Elmer Blotno, whose weekly column in *The Future* pontificates on just about every subject connected to literature. Blotno has always ignored Tarassiev's work, but on November 18, 2048, the following title unfurls above his august byline: "The end of the hero according to Bogdan Tarrasiev." It is an article without much substance, but written with verve and good spirits, and in short, Blotno lavishes praise on Tarassiev's procedure, dubbing it "hoaxish." Blotno uses the opportunity to give the impression that he regularly reads the small journals—a bold-faced lie—and that he has read *Ransacked* as well as "Tarassiev's recent novels"—second lie. His reflections are fashionable. They rely on dispersed material, impossible to find in bookstores and unknown to *The Future's* readers. Their goal is not to bring a previously unknown genius into the limelight. But they do constitute a sort of birth certificate into the literary world. It's a fundamental piece in the author's razor-thin press file.

Soon Tarassiev submits the *Wolff* manuscript to Lambda Press. Blotno's review has intervened in *Wolff's* favor more than the sublime qualities of the book, and the editor, who has long since ceased to believe in the necessity of publishing an author like Tarassiev, relents. *Wolff's* release is scheduled for September 2049.

Wolff is a vast testamentary work, where all of Bogdan Tarassiev's talents come together harmoniously: the art of epic monologue, portrayal of dark scenes, oscillation between political and mystical spheres, biting humor, nested story lines, tangled interior worlds, portrayal of the drift towards madness or death. In it we see an old man, nearly blind, who wanders across landscapes of his century—and in particular, an immense, bombed-out metropolis, transparent allusion to the war of 2038—as he searches for the precise moment when the bifurcation towards the irremediable took place. Each time he identifies such a node, often appearing in the form of one or more beings, he attempts to dream a dream in which those responsible for misfortune are destroyed, shot down, or rendered unable to cause harm. It goes without saying that his mode of acting on real history proves ineffective.

The year 2049 is a period when Tarassiev has conquered a well-defined place in the literary landscape: that of a minor writer, whose novels nobody has read, whose fiction can't be placed, but whose

name is known because it becomes associated with an easily cari-
catured writer's tic: "that guy who gives all his characters the same
name."

Buoyed by this minute movement of interest, *Wolff* appears in
bookstores without being completely overshadowed. Still, the arsenal
deployed to defend the book and make it known remain quite weak:
three summaries, two articles in cuisine and craft magazines, where
the freelancers associated with the small journals have a derisory right
to express themselves freely, and an invitation to a radio roundtable
on "Writers and the Global Situation." In *The Future*, Elmer Blotno
has not deigned to renew his support of Tarassiev, and the minuscule
article on *Wolff*, signed R. R., is woefully bland. Tarassiev's path can
be measured in sales figures: for the first time since *Encounter with
the Infanta*, they pass the five hundred-copy mark.

The critics' tepidity is manifest, the public's alienation is patent,
and Lambda Press announces to Tarassiev that the disappointing
publishing adventure begun five years earlier ends with *Wolff*.

From then on, Bogdan Tarassiev no longer has an editor, and
moreover, he no longer works on lengthy books. He suffers physically; his breathing, because of inflammation spreading below his
sternum, is increasingly difficult; his joints are painful, transforming
everyday activity into martyrdom. He publishes four more stories in
journals, incorporating characters named Wlaff, Wolff, and Wulwo.
They are fantasy novellas, surrealist, and always completely at odds
with the taste, the styles, the fads, the ideological touchstones of official literature. Without going overboard here in pompous apprecia-
tion, they can be considered magnificent texts.

One of these novellas, called *Opus 24*, presents a writer, Jacob
Wulwo, who has more than one trait in common with Tarassiev,
although his destiny and method of working are different. Jacob
Wulwo is part of a small armed force that skillfully assassinates international crime bosses, pimps, political directors, and the makers of
anti-personnel mines. Alongside this praiseworthy vigilante activity,
he writes minimalist novels whose characters act in stereotyped ways,
without differentiating themselves from one another; they dress the
same way, have the same motivations, the same miserable social

status, say the same things, profess the same beliefs, etc. From one novel to another, Jacob Wulwo tells the same anecdote—a sordid love story—without worrying about embellishing it with variations.

"I think that what we have here," Bogdan Tarassiev comments in an author's note, "is a literary procedure intended to problematize the limits of creativity in fictional works, but which also indicates an active disdain for writing itself, a sort of self-mutilation intended to ridicule and degrade the notion of the book, the notion of the author, and the false values that are associated with them; we must take it as a demonstration of hostility in which are mixed equal parts disgust with writing and hatred of the official publishing world."

These four texts appear in 2050 and in 2052. At that time, Tarassiev's aura is definitively extinguished everywhere. In 2050, a young and hallucinatory editor, Roman Nachtigall, expresses the desire to collect the scattered and inaccessible stories into a single volume, but the project doesn't take off.

Once again enveloped in silence, Tarssiev no longer has any discernible social existence. In a postcard to a female friend, he admits that he is in the midst of editing a pamphlet against Western society, but nothing of it will be discovered in his papers after his death. Tarassiev most certainly destroyed all of his unpublished works, but it's also possible that he renounced writing, with the exception of the brief untitled text that undoubtedly constitutes his last opus, *Opus 25*—a text about which we will now say a few words.

Bogdan Tarassiev's doctor, Igor Mundrian, is a medical consultant often called upon by the TV station UM5. He hosts a quarterly medical show on the channel. During a discussion on dermatoses, he invites Tarassiev to come and explain live on the air the challenges that his psoriasis causes for his joints. Tarassiev will be announced as a patient gravely afflicted, but also, Mundrian affirms, as a "literary personality"—the show's objective being to show that the illness strikes indiscriminately and democratically everyday people as well as stars, with Bogdan Tarassiev playing the role of star. For unknown reasons, undoubtedly out of morose masochism, Tarassiev accepts the invitation to appear on Mundrian's show.

And so on July 12, 2053, Tarassiev makes a television appearance as an author. It's the first time that this medium has welcomed him. In 2053, Bogdan Tarassiev looks like an old man whose movements are constantly slowed by problems of cartilage, bones and tissues in the midst of petrification. His physiognomy recalls that of the physicist Einstein, although he wears glasses and his gaze is even more dreamlike than Einstein's. After a short introduction by a presenter who reminds the audience in a suave voice that Tarassiev has written "several very beautiful novels on the theme of illness and psoriasis", he has the floor for four and a half minutes. In actuality, he must respond to Mundrian's precise clinical questions. He does it with a certain grace, employing humorous turns of phrase that make him immediately likable. Let's say, to sum up, that his televised performance is good and pleases the audience.

During the summer of 2053, the consequences of this stint in UM5's studios make themselves known: UM5 offers him a spot on the show *Winnie's Fifteen Minutes*, on the topic of "Writers and Psoriasis"; two associations, SOS-Dermatosis and Genetic-Assistance, offer admittance to their sponsorship committees; and as for the rich, humanitarian, and quasi-governmental organization Life-Boat, he is invited to its traditional September gala, at which representatives of political and media high society gather for a family back-to-school photo. Tarassiev responds in the affirmative to all of these solicitations. The first to become concrete is that of Life-Boat.

On September 14, 2053, armed with a crutch and an orthopedic apparatus designed to facilitate the movement of his right arm, Bogdan Tarassiev wanders around the grounds of City Hall, where the tents and tables of the prestigious Life-Boat cocktail party have been set up. The guests, dressed in formal attire, are numerous. Women wear designer gowns. Jewels are on display and gleaming. Celebrities pass in front of cameras and make speeches in which they call listeners to fight against poverty, to support altruism, and to give hefty donations.

It's cloudy and a bit cool, but it's not raining. A small plate in his hand, Tarassiev hobbles between groups in which he knows no one. He is a complete outsider in this society. Tarassiev's universe, whether in his fiction or in his real life, has never intersected with the sphere of luxury, has never approached the social strata that swarm with the smiling faces of the happy people of the world, those who govern the planet and who, supposedly in passing, imagine that their governance is good and generous. He has talked about them, but always while placing them beyond an uncrossable chasm, out of the intellectual reach of his narrators, just as masters of horror evoke the horrible without describing it. His heroes are often killers, men and women who preach pitiless elimination of "those responsible for misfortune," but, aside from a few murder scenes that are more fantasy than realism, the narratives don't explore the concrete spaces where the powerful prevail. Due to a visceral antipathy, but also with the sentiment that for him such representation would be mentally and literarily impossible, Tarassiev never worries about activating any sort of believable image of the rich, even at the moment when they're killed, even at the moment when he, as the author, kills them. He accompanies his victims into violent death breath after breath, but it almost never strikes anyone but the creatures at the bottom of the social ladder, and even of the human ladder.

Nonetheless, here Bogdan Tarassiev rubs shoulders with people whom his characters, his madmen and his ideologically deviant wretches, have always designated as targets. He sets down his plate on which a few crumbs of salmon crisp remain, he grabs a glass of champagne, undoubtedly of fine vintage, and he drinks it. Then he heads towards a fairly loud group, in the middle of which he recognizes a minister of the Republic. He approaches, takes out a Colt, and, with clear intention, shoots the minister (Ando Baltcharol, Minister of Industrial Development), two Secretaries of State (Dadzor Adamiyaz, Solidarity, and Werner Wens, Refugees and Camp Administration), as well as two other people whom he wounds slightly. Then he turns the weapon on himself and blows his brains out.

This was fifty years ago.

Bogdan Tarassiev's *Opus 25* can serve as a conclusion to this study. We don't pretend to have fully identified Bogdan Tarassiev's personality, but perhaps we will have succeeded at drawing attention to an extraordinary body of work, which nonetheless remains unknown even today: unfairly, and unfortunately.

Tarassiev's *Opus 25* presents itself as a folded sheet of paper inside a bloody envelope. The blood, in theory, is not part of the work. The paper contains just one sentence. It was found in Tarassiev's wallet. Its content was disseminated widely, taken up by the press along with information about "the September fourteenth killings." Counting this final and brief poetic manifestation, and if we recall the first volumes that appeared under the name of Balbaïan, we can consider that all of Bogdan Tarassiev's works of fiction were, for better or worse, published.

Here's the sentence, which investigators judged to be enigmatic, but which now, for readers of this article, seems less so, and which undoubtedly, for some among us, is of an absolute clarity:

"If you desire that your journey to death may take on its full meaning, if you wish to know why you remained silent, do as I do. Wolff."

THE THEORY OF THE IMAGE ACCORDING TO MARIA THREE-THIRTEEN

SHE RUNS BREATHLESSLY straight ahead, or in the direction that she believes to be forward. She's more or less sure of having a name, perhaps Maria Three-Thirteen, or in any case Maria or Mariya, and an age, twenty-nine years old. Or fifty-nine. The precise figure escapes her. She feels the darkness that streams across her skin, that spreads out as it encounters her face. It combines with the air to flow over her like a light fluid, bland and tepid, that offers little resistance and that terrifies her as soon as she thinks of it. It's a violent shadow, without the faintest suggestion of future light. She feels it settle on her at each step, at each jolt of her moving body. She has a hard time catching her breath and she is aware that she is inhaling a bizarre substance that belongs to the depths and to nightmares. A gas that transports primarily ugliness and sooty stagnation. And since she's running nude, her immediate impressions are poisoned by the embarrassment that her nudity provokes in her. She's desolate. And everything repulses her. Everything that brushes against her. She has never felt much affinity for naturism, nor, in short, for her own body. In her lifetime, she has avoided exposing herself in the nude as much as possible. And now, although she knows that here no gaze can evaluate her physically or sexually, although she does not fear the heavy, offensive perversity of voyeurism on her, she feels horribly uncomfortable. Running in the dark is a trial that few people can face in a relaxed manner, even when everything is ruined, even after their death. You have to force yourself not to constantly think about the obstacles that rise up on the road with no warning, about the devastating collisions that are always possible, about hideous encounters, about holes and ravines. And it's better not to think about the nature of the ground. Here it could be compared to a hardened sand, crusty, that doesn't injure the ball of the foot and is pleasantly elastic, but at the same time it evokes some unknown organic tissue, motionless and repellant. To understand what's really at stake, you have to go into dreams or into death. A wave of repulsion passes through the runner's legs, it rises towards her belly, towards her lower abdomen. Naturists may claim that one feels free and happy when the body is rid of all clothing, but Maria Three-Thirteen does not find any greater well-being; on the contrary. Her flesh flops around in a manner that she considers humiliating and, moreover, almost painful. She feels darkness enter her through every opening of her body. These openings that a lama should have closed this morning with wax and cotton, once the death had been verified, which is precisely what he didn't do, for destiny opposed it. The memories of her last moments come to her then fade before they can become believable elements. Everything grows further away, everything remained behind her, nothing precise lasts. Images persist, but it takes an enormous effort for her memory to identify and fix them in place. Maria Three-Thirteen pushes this work off for later. She's concentrating on the present, which is to say on her physical activity. She runs with long strides, and in order to keep her balance, she fights above all against the sensations of disgust that invade her. She knows practically nothing anymore, she only knows that she has been running for awhile, ten minutes, perhaps, or for several hours. Or for an even longer time. There are no reliable landmarks. Here time passes by following paths that no one has ever explored. Here the hands of a clock would undoubtedly behave like needles on a compass at the North Pole. Maria Three-Thirteen doesn't think about that, she refuses to suffer from the incoherence or the absence of duration. The problem no longer interests her. Up until her death, she would have been sensitive to it, but now, what matters is found elsewhere. She keeps up her momentum, making a point to conserve the same rhythm. She has a stitch in her side but she tries to ignore it.

But she has slowed down a bit. She's in pain.

Then she stops.

She's winded. She knows that she must speak. She can't easily find her words. First her breath passing through her throat becomes audible. Then syllables form. Nothing at all can be seen.

I am late, says Maria Three-Thirteen.

Nobody answers her. Nobody reacts. Before her, in the thick shadows that nothing will ever again soften, in this total blackness, it's as though she had no interlocutor.

Excuse me, she says. I was delayed. The lama who was supposed to wash my body and seal its orifices had a heart attack at precisely the moment that he entered the morgue. It was his destiny and it was mine. My body remained without care. After such an unlucky turn of events, I had to take the initiative myself to come to you. I know that it is a paltry excuse, but I have no other. Forgive me, too, for not furnishing more details. I don't know the name of the monk who was struck down, I don't know offhand the address of the medical-legal institute to which I was transferred from my cell, I have forgotten the number of my original cell and I no longer remember the events that marked my final night.

She hesitates.

All that has slipped my mind, she says. I don't know if it will come back or if the amnesia is permanent. Nobody told me anything. Usually, one benefits from the monk's assistance for several days. The monk's voice is there, nearby. It doesn't ring out all the time, and it's hard to hear, and often you don't understand, but it's reassuring.

She hesitates again.

But, in my case, nothing. The monk collapsed on the threshold of the room with the refrigerated compartments, and he died, or, at least, he will not speak again. He was taken somewhere else. I had to do without his services. This is my destiny.

In front of her, nothing moves.

This is my destiny, she repeats.

The silence is as limitless as the night's opacity, and as soon as she ceases to break it with breath and word, it closes in around her, against her, and within earshot and all the way to the horizon.

I came as fast as I could, she resumes.

Her panting breath in the dark.

The sound of saliva in her throat.

The minuscule wheezings of her alveoli.

She breathes noisily, discouraged, crushed, ashamed of being naked and upright facing her audience. She knows she must speak. Everything is obscene, death with consciousness, and her nudity, and the murmurings that her organs produce, and her posture of a madwoman stopped before the unknown, before strangers and nothingness, and her mouth and her orifices unsealed after death, and, to give herself composure and not shout out or sob from terror, or let herself be overcome by anguish, she knows that all that remains for her is to speak.

When she was alive, before her long stays in special prisons and antiterrorist penitentiaries, she wrote fairytales and prose pieces, and then, accompanied by the men and women detained with her, she continued to narrate, to murmur, to vociferate, and to ruminate. And suddenly, without having to rummage through her memory, she remembers one of her very first texts. She hadn't thought of it during all these interminable years of incarceration, undoubtedly because it was a story like all teenagers compose, unfinished and ungainly, but here, without warning and for no reason, the text appears again. And she's immediately struck by its premonitory nature. Between the absurd situation that she described in it and what she's in the midst of confronting, commonalities abound.

Several creatures wake up, semi-human and semi-animal, seated on a tribunal dais. Their memory doesn't give them any self-knowledge, they know nothing about the affair that they must judge, nor even about the world where they've landed. The only landmark they have at their disposal is the individual lamp that illuminates a bit of the table before them. The darkness all around is without hope. Silence reigns, crushing, and prolongs itself. Aware that the situation must be untangled in one way or another, they all imagine being observed by their neighbors with discontent and even with hatred. In reality, all share, without knowing it, a vertiginous feeling of guilt and solitude. The strangeness of the situation reinforces itself every moment; immobility grows stronger. The minutes flow, more and more painful. The only way to put an end to the unbearable seems to be to take the floor. Their voice must be heard, they must seem to take on their judiciary function competently. After having cleared its throat, the massive animal who is in the middle, and who therefore assumes the need to play the role of president, opens the dossier placed in front of it and begins to read it with a thundering voice. Startled by the excessive vibration of its vocal cords, painfully embarrassed by the words it pronounces, it nonetheless continues its speech. What it has before it is a prose poem, surrealist, a completely incongruous text. The creatures sitting to its left and its right have collapsed at the idea that they must now prove their existence and therefore respond. In order not to underscore its own foreignness to the world, each one in turn pretends to know the procedure and intervenes, masking its fears under an aggressive excess of confidence. The readings follow one after the other. The poems are not always of a trivial nature and, on the contrary, abound in imprecations and personal attacks; however, they are formulated in a sufficiently obscure manner that each magistrate feels deeply implicated. The tribunal session has no end. The nightmare has no escape.

Maria Three-Thirteen remembers this text almost word for word, and it's not of a nature to reassure her. It's out of the question for her to read it aloud. On the other hand, she feels a sort of disquisition on the tip of her tongue. She is not going to start reciting post-exotic or surrealist poems, but she has a vague sense that what's presenting itself to her is a strange speech.

Excuse me if what I'm about to say is a bit disjointed, she apologizes. I was notified only yesterday that a conference would take place here and that I was invited to make remarks. I haven't had time to prepare. This is not my area of expertise. Until today, I focused on the creation of little fairytales, and the repetition of narracts and stories that the men and women who were my fellow prisoners transmitted. I rarely let myself go with reflections on the origins of language and the philosophy of nothingness.

She lets a moment pass. Then she begins again.

Please go easy on me, she says.

She hasn't yet fully recovered her breath, and despite the absolute darkness, her nakedness continues to make her suffer. She doesn't protect the base of her pubis with her left hand, she doesn't place her right arm in front of her nipples, but she ceaselessly thinks of her immodestly undressed body, which she doesn't know how to cover.

I am not very sure that my reflections will suit you, she resumes. I have always been oriented towards fiction, you know. Towards political pamphlets and fiction. Before prison, I mainly composed poems and strange little narratives. Nothing that really sold well. And then, in the high-security penitentiaries, I was in touch with post-exotic writers and shamans, with men and women and insane people like Ingrid Schmitz, Maria Schrag, and Liliane Oregone, and together we created a literature that has no name.

She breathes in and breathes out as best she can a few times before continuing her monologue.

A vast literature that touched on nearly every subject and every genre, she says next, but that has no name. I am not sure that my remarks fit into this frame. I will try not to disappoint you. I will endeavor to make myself understood. But I guarantee nothing. My presentation may resemble the speech of an insane person or the speech of the dying. Please do not hold it against me.

She quiets down, awaiting a reaction in front of her. She listens carefully. Nobody, at any distance, bothers to give her a signal. It's as though she were irretrievably alone.

For several moments, she tries to catch a mental glimpse of what she will say, but nothing presents itself to her. It's as though she's at the edge of a black abyss. She must launch herself into the void to know more.

She's standing up to her ankles in a barely tepid dust.

Not a single echo breaks the compact silence.

Not a single breath.

All that is audible are the noises that her naked body produces. Rumbles, beats, and wheezes.

Once again, humiliation causes her to despair. Being without clothing, being alone, being dead and having to speak to give the impression that she can tolerate her current situation.

Nobody can see anything at all, she says. Something moves in my mouth and passes beyond it and becomes words. I hear that which ruptures the silence and I have no reason to be proud of it. But it's my voice, or, in any case, a vibration that comes from my mouth, and I can't remove myself from it or be unaware of it.

She would like to sit or crouch down. But, for the moment, she senses that doing so would mean adopting an even more obscene posture relative to her audience.

Whoever you are, you have been patient in waiting for me, and I thank you, she says. I thank you in advance for your attention.

Then she breathes in, she thinks one last time of the unhappy creature in her first novel, who opened an unknown folder and read it in a pompous voice without understanding anything in it. And she launches into it. She makes her speech.

The word, she begins. The very beginning.

In the beginning, at least in our post-exotic world, in the beginning there is no word. There is no word but there is a bit of light, and even if there is no light there is the image of a place and of a situation, and only the image matters. Only the image becomes clear from the beginning and imposes itself. It is stable, it has all its importance from the beginning, it is sufficient in itself and could be sufficient for us.

The voice comes in addition, it comes after, it is added, for example it's a commentary that's located outside the image, an external literary intervention. An added, artificial intervention. It hardly interests us. Or, second possibility, it's a voice that's born in the image and that transforms the image into the stage of a spectacle, into a theatrical stage, with monologues, dialogues, and songs. This second voice interests us. But often it's neither one nor the other.

Neither commentary nor theatrical murmur. Neither one nor the other.

Maria Three-Thirteen lets several seconds lapse.

In certain cases, she picks up again, which is to say often, this voice that comes after is a voice that belongs to the image, that surges from who knows what depths of the image, and that is the very expression of the image, the linguistic expression of the image.

I will name this voice the deaf voice, but I think that it could also be called the natural voice. It is natural because it assumes forces, natural forces that belong to the image, that don't need human language or human vocal cords in order to express themselves. It is natural because it relies on that which exists in the image, that which really, concretely exists, because it relies on that which pre-exists and is not the fruit of an external intervention or even just an observation. It is natural because its loudspeakers are elements that are natural to the image, elements like the wind, or animals, or abandoned objects, or like old objects or bits of cloth that are themselves laden with memories, or again, another example, other natural elements in the image, other natural loudspeakers, like mute characters or dead people.

The image speaks with a deaf voice. It says things in a continuous way from the very beginning and without the word. It pronounces things in its non-human language and in its not truly vocal language, it articulates things with its voice without vocal cords. It's only later that actors and actresses intervene, only later that characters speak with their vibrating voices, who mutely utter the world or who keep quiet.

Maria Three-Thirteen closes her eyes, then she opens them again. Outside of her, there has not been a single change. She wonders if anyone is listening to her. She dreams again of her skin and her unsealed orifices, of her openings that no fabric conceals, and for several seconds this thought demoralizes her, then she forces herself to make an effort and plunges back into her lecture. An example, she thinks. Give an example, Maria Three-Thirteen. An example or an anecdote. Otherwise the audience may scatter.

January 22, 2007, she says, Yasar Tarchalski exited his interior obscurity and entered a dream. The dream was painful, as almost always happens when you've been transferred, when you've changed floors and when you know it will take months of listening and groping before melting into the community of voices in your new environment, for, even when you've previously known the men and women imprisoned in the neighboring cells, it takes time to float without problems from one to the other. You'd like to be one with them quickly, adopt without difficulty the personality of each detainee to restore life to her when she is dying or to pay homage to her when she has died, one would like to adopt their style, their temperament, and their obsessions as a man or as a woman. But Yasar Tarchalski had been transferred several hours earlier, he spent his first night in cell 501 and he hadn't yet been able to contact his neighbors in the closest cells. And so his dream was painful.

His dream was painful and it consisted above all of a situation and an image. Yasar Tarchalski wore military attire and he walked on a concrete esplanade along the sea. Beyond the concrete there was nothing but empty kiosks, and, beyond that, there was nothing. The image spoke; without a human voice it told Yasar Tarchalski that he had taken the wrong path, that his destination was not on the maps and that the railway that he planned to follow had been shifted by several dozen kilometers. It said this in its deaf voice. The language of the image penetrated Tarchalski and he understood that he would not be able to reach in time the convoy that he should have reached before evening. He zigzagged between puddles that reflected the very gray and very bright sky, then he went to the edge of the esplanade and began climbing a first flight of steps. Now the sea was very far below him. He moved reluctantly along the vertical wall, with the precipice to his right. He didn't have vertigo but he was breathing noisily and with difficulty, for he knew that he hadn't taken the right path. The narrow stairway led him towards a glass-enclosed shelter with most of its windowpanes broken by wind and age. Several people had taken refuge there, half a dozen men and women whom Yasar Tarchalski had known, alongside whom he had fought, and whom he hadn't seen for a quarter of a century. They were on this platform leaning against the wall, overlooking the sea, with no exit. Anguish left them mute. Tarchalski went and merged with them. The image continued to speak, it told them that they had no exit, that time was passing, and that there was no point in hoping or even continuing.

Suddenly, Yasar Tarchalski began to speak. I remember his phrase very precisely. "And you, Ilitch," he said, "did you ever think that perhaps it would never happen, even in a thousand years?" Nobody in the group was named Ilitch. All of us grew considerably more anguished.

Yasar Tarchalski didn't take long to wake up. Ilitch who? he immediately thought. What was I talking about with this voice? Whose was this voice that passed through my mouth?

Sweating, he tossed and turned on the concrete slab that served as a bed in his new cell, then he got up. Everyone on the floor was sleeping. Below, someone shouted, then quieted down.

"And you, Ilitch," Tarchalski repeated, "did you ever think that perhaps it would never happen, even in a thousand years?" He murmured it in an oppressed tone, facing the door, his head almost touching the bars in front of the door's hatch. What did it mean, he thought, what was it that could never happen, even in a thousand years? He closed his eyes to try and observe his dream once again through his memories. He saw all the people in the group, but the image no longer spoke and he himself had become fuzzy.

"Who said that?" he shouted through the hatch. "Which voice spoke earlier? Which voice spoke to Ilitch earlier?"

He pounded his fist against the door. Nobody responded.

"Whose voice was it?" he croaked again.

Then he was quiet.

Maria Three-Thirteen is winded and she has the impression that her vertical position, artificial and possibly provocative, worthy of a pornographic magazine for the blind, is no longer really suited to the circumstances. She hesitates, she is just about to drop close to the ground, to crouch down, then she resists the desire and remains upright. Crouched, legs spread, even if the shadows formed a screen that would temper the obscenity of her pose, crouched would be worse.

She waits for the rest to come. Her breathing is irregular. Then, after a minute passes, her lungs calm down.

Once again, words prepare to leave her mouth. She opens her mouth slightly and they come out.

As we have just seen, she says, uncertainty is great when it comes to determining the origin of voices. Characters within an image often succeed at gathering enough strength to speak, sometimes in the form of a monologue, sometimes in the form of a dialogue, but the darkness in them and around them is such that one cannot definitively confirm who has really spoken. They themselves do not ask the question, but, when they do ask it, they feel incapable of responding. They do not know the response, or rather they are not one hundred percent sure. They base it on probabilities. They identify a familiar voice that expresses thoughts or bits of thoughts that don't shock them, thoughts with which they spontaneously agree, or perhaps this voice releases lies or fragments of lies that help them out. And they deduce from it that they are in the midst of speaking, there is agitation at the level of their mouth and they deduce from it that, probably, they are in the midst of speaking. They recognize a voice that seems to correspond to that which they have always imagined to be their own, and they take the step, they overcome their hesitation and they decide that it is indeed their voice that they hear, their voice that sighs banalities or falsehoods in the depths of the darkness, in the depths of the thick darkness. Nevertheless, it happens that doubt insinuates itself in them. This situation happens especially when the voice that they would like to claim for themselves resounds somewhere in their skull while they have their mouth closed and so everything would suggest that they are silent, sleeping, or dead. It's in those moments that uncertainty grows. They are painful moments. The character is startled. Whether it's a man or a woman, they are startled. Suddenly they realize that someone else, very close to them, has perhaps borrowed their voice, or that something or even someone has forced them to speak from who knows what depths of their skull. I can say from experience that this interrogation elicits an increase in the amount of adrenaline in the blood, when one still has blood, and a painful feeling of anguish, when one still has feelings. One inquires into the origin of one's own voice and doesn't find any satisfactory response anywhere in oneself. You flinch and groan several discontented words as an aside, and you interrupt yourself, sometimes mid-sentence. If the darkness is really dense, you cough to clear your throat and wait for what follows. You cough to clear your throat, you say nothing else, you crouch in the darkness, on the very dark ground, and wait for what follows.

She coughs to clear her throat. She says nothing else. She crouches in the shadows, a few inches above the frighteningly powdery and black ground, then she gets up again, shocked that she was not able to resist this movement, then, after muttering and dithering, she lowers herself again and she sits on her heels. It's a more natural posture at least, even if she looks risqué, a posture that is more conducive to the circumstances than staying planted on her feet like an animal standing on its hind legs, bizarrely frozen in front of nothingness.

Images, she thinks. I must make my demonstration less abstract. Maria Three-Thirteen, it's imperative that you manage to provide illustrations that they can recognize. Otherwise they'll get distracted. Otherwise they'll think of nothing besides my sex and my orifices.

And now, she begins again, to illustrate, I will cite a few images without words or almost without words, several images that make their deaf voice heard. You know them, you have certainly attended cinema showings during which they've been projected before you. These are not immobile images, but they are fundamentally silent, and they make their deaf voice heard very strongly.

- The chess match with death in *The Seventh Seal* by Ingmar Bergman, with, in the background, a procession of silhouettes that undertake the arduous ascent of a hill.
- The man on all fours who barks in the mud facing a dog in *Damnation* by Béla Tarr.
- The baby that cries in a sordid and windowless apartment in *Eraserhead* by David Lynch.
- The bare façade of an abandoned apartment building, with *Nosferatu's* head in a window, in Nosferatu by Friedrich Murnau.
- The boat that moves away across an empty sea, overflowing with cadavers, at the end of *Shame* by Ingmar Bergman.
- The desert landscape, half hidden by a curtain that the wind lifts in *Ashes of Time* by Wong Kar Wai.
- The early morning travel by handcar, with the regular sound of the wheels, in *Stalker* by Andrei Tarkovsky.
- The old man with cancer who sings on a swing in *Ikiru* by Akira Kurosawa.
- The blind dwarfs with their enormous motorcycle glasses who hit each other with canes in *Even Dwarfs Started Small* by Werner Herzog.

- The train station where three bandits wait at the beginning of *Once Upon a Time in the West* by Sergio Leone.
- The flares above the river in *Ivan's Childhood* by Andrei Tarkovsky.
- The prairie traveled over by a gust of wind in *The Mirror* by Andrei Tarkovsky.

She is quiet for a moment.

There are many others, she thinks. They all speak. They all speak without language, with a deaf voice, with a natural and deaf voice.

When the image appears there cannot be silence, she begins again. Even when the darkness is complete, even when the image is black and nobody rustles or speaks, there cannot be silence. A voice rises up and it carries something other than the language of the mouth and even something other than moments of cries, breaths, or murmurs. It carries memories, memories of images, memories of the body. It speaks in the deaf voice of the image or in the voice of the body. The body that speaks out of the thick darkness of the image, and that sometimes even speaks from beneath the image, speaks with its language of the body that is without words but that is also without silence. It can happen that the body that speaks will take a break, but globally it is without silence. The deaf voice of the image passes around it and in this voice there are almost constantly memories of the body that it attracts to itself and that it appropriates. When the deaf voice of the image has abandoned its memories of the body, the body takes them to itself and speaks of them with its voice of the body. The memories branch out in silence or the absence of silence until they become moments of cries or moments of breath or of murmurs, and until the body has had enough of the memories to be able to be quiet. These are not necessarily memories of suffering and they are not necessarily human. But, even when they are numerous enough to constitute a character or a story that is dissociated from the image, even when the voice of the body is quiet, it remains distanced from silence, it lets itself be traversed by the deaf voice of the image and it remains distanced from its own silence.

She stops lecturing. She feels terribly tired. It also seems to her that she hasn't listened to what was coming out of her mouth. It's one more unpleasant sensation. She waddles from one foot to the other, like a too-heavy bird trying to find a good position atop her eggs. Then she relaxes. She doesn't move anymore.

Talk about the depths, she thinks. I won't be understood at all if I don't talk about the depths.

She tries to remember what she has just said to her mute audience, to her audience perhaps devoid of existence. She would be incapable of repeating it. And those whom she has somehow addressed, have they retained the terms of her lesson, or at least a few snippets? She scrutinizes what is very close, what is in the distance. Nothing is distinct. Everything is indifferently drowned in a pitch that no glimmer of light will ever pierce. She would like to see or touch something, but she finds herself surrounded by absence. Aside from the sooty ground, there is nothing she can close her fingers around. An almost inanimate and completely vapid air descends on her body.

Her lungs pulls it into her, then send it into the shadows.

She wonders if, now, after all this time, she is emitting odors. The idea that she could be giving off pestilence, even limited, horrifies her. My orifices, she thinks. Nothing says that they won't start expelling the body's stenches, whiffs. Whiffs of viscera. Nothing says that my orifices haven't already started to spit stench. For a minute, she tries to sniff her own odors. She smells nothing, but the shame of being nauseating, in the heart of the shadows, grows stronger. She moves a bit, she dances from one leg to the other, then, once again, she relaxes. Later, she thinks. My speech is not finished. I will tackle the question of the depths.

I must talk about the depths, she reminds herself.

In the depths, image does not yet exist, she begins again. There is only a blackishness. In the depths of the night or in the depths of despair, no matter. The blackishness crouches in the darkness and grumbles, trying to pronounce something that will remove it from solitude or unconsciousness. The blackishness is alone, at the very bottom, and grumbles. Grumbles or mutters. The deaf voice undoubtedly comes from this solitude and this muttering. In the beginning, there is not even the image yet, there are only the depths and the shadow, and there is a blind blackishness, hunched over, that mutters about its current non-existence and about its existence to come. It is not yet the image, it is not yet the deaf voice, and at any rate, the word does not yet exist. The deaf voice is without word and that which moves within the grumbling is without language and without word. Fairly often, I myself crouch down like that to mutter to the depths of the night or the depths of despair, and I know that then there is no image, that image does not yet exist. My testimony counts. You are in the depths, head between the arms, folded in on yourself to the point of pain, without word and without language, and you know well that you are far from any image. You grumble without words, you mutter, nothing is said, nothing is seen, deaf or not the voice carries nowhere, the darkness retains nothing. It is not yet the image and it is not even the absence of the image.

Yes, she thinks. Yes, that's it. I must continue to talk about that. I don't understand half of it, but it must pass beyond me. I grumble without words, I mutter, nothing is said, nothing is seen, but something passes beyond me. Deaf or not, my voice carries nowhere. The darkness retains nothing. But it's my voice. I must continue to say it.

The voice of characters often comes from their chest rather than from their skull, she continues. It passes through the dark red matter of their lungs, through the pipes of vicious and uncertain colors like those of jellyfish and the cartilage of cadavers, then it trembles on the reddish vocal cords that are, let's be honest, breathtakingly ugly, an ugliness matched only by that of the tongue and the inside of the mouth when they are examined from inside, for instance when you have just emerged at the top of the pharynx and you're already moving towards the teeth and the lips. The voice of characters takes an essentially red path and leaves the body after a very nasty walk through red flesh. It's in this red matter of the chest and the base of the head that it takes its origin. It doesn't come from the brain and it's only at the moment when it flows back towards it, in order to inform it of its existence, it's only at that moment that the gray matter receives it, adopts it, and makes it believe that it was born in its breast, close to it, in its grayness. Obediently, the voice of characters prides itself in having its origin in gray intelligence and gray consciousness. But, in reality, it's only after its red path that it evolves towards a level of language that moves beyond the cry or the murmur. In reality, it was first a voice of the chest, a voice of red tissues and red bodies. The voice of characters lays claim to the intelligent and conscious grayness, but, in the depths, it was always red, and sometimes it remembers and conceals it, sometimes it remembers and it doesn't hide it, and sometimes, too, it doesn't remember anything, and it vibrates miserably, in the intelligence and the consciousness, in the grayness. Miserably.

One more memory, says Maria Three-Thirteen.
Nobody knows exactly if it's really she who speaks or if what is heard is pronounced by another character or even by another author. But it is her voice.
One more memory, she repeats.

I found myself inside the image, she says. Black all around, and, as soon as I closed my eyes, a landscape of high plateaus, an immense plain with hardly any contour, crushed by the sky all the way to the horizon. The grasses rippled, shimmering and velvety dull or bright green, depending on the gusts of wind, depending on the moods of the wind in the distance. With such a light, with the ocean of grasses all around, one wonders what there could have been to say. I was inside the image, I was alone and I was saying nothing, and from time to time, I opened my eyes and I took a step or two. My hands immediately encountered the walls of my cell, or the door, whose metal was almost lukewarm. I could have said what my hands touched when I opened my eyes, but I didn't feel like it and I was calling my memories to mind in order to say something else. My memory failed me, as it often does. I couldn't remember anything but the immediate present, which is to say the image in which I found myself as soon as my eyelids lowered, this immense Mongolian sky that was married by the grasses to the immense Mongolian earth. The deaf voice of the image passed through me. It said to me that I had the voice of a person and even of a character and that I could use this voice to speak my existence, to tell my past or recent or present or invented existence and to speak the image.

I spoke the image.

I closed my eyes and I opened them, I didn't know if I existed in the past or in something else, I didn't know if I was dead or alive before being in the image. I had the voice of a person. I used it to be a character and I held myself in a vertical position, like humans do, under the Mongolian sky that was crushing me. The grasses rippled and there was basically nothing to say. I observed long silences and, whether I closed or opened my eyes, almost no sound left my mouth.

There you have it, she thinks.

She doesn't know whether sounds are leaving her mouth or not. She has the impression that they are, but, out of lassitude, she doesn't bother to verify by listening to what happens in the silence. She settles in a bit closer to the ground. She pictures herself as she truly is, crouched near the formidably black dust, insignificant in the heart of the shadows. Maria Three-Thirteen, she thinks, you are no longer anything, not even a voice. What does it matter whether or not you have deaf and mute listeners before you. If they are males, they do not see you, they confuse you with the rest of the blackness, they do not distinguish any of your corporeal or mental details. If they are females, they have no reason to observe you with malevolence, and, in any case, they don't care. What does it matter whether or not you spread your eyelids or your legs.

She stays this way for a long time, exhausted near the neither warm nor cold ground, not manifesting herself in any way.

There you have it, she says again.

There are also voices that are born without the image, and that violently stir up verbal hallucinations from which only then can one imagine images. These are the vociferous voices. The vociferous voices don't belong to characters and neither do they have their origin in the image. Vociferous voices don't appear in the space or the time of the image, they don't travel along the red path at the interior of the body that goes from the breath to the mouth, and neither do they obey the grayness of the gray matter, the gray intelligence, the gray memory, the gray consciousness. The vociferous voices are like post-exoticism, they come from elsewhere and they go nowhere or they go elsewhere. You hear them, but they speak among themselves, which is to say they speak to no one. They vociferate for themselves, they stir up their rhythms outside of everything, they project their violence and their flashes outside of everything. In the universe they briefly deposit images devoid of the deaf voice, or of cries without breath, or of bits of hermetic memory. The vociferous voices are foreigners to the world of characters and to the world of images. They have a language folded in on itself, a language of hermetic nightmare, and they do not mix with the image. They do not mix either with the deaf voice of the image, or with the image.

When the voice vociferates, it thinks of humble and terrible animals, it thinks of the flames of war and the flames of ovens where they burn humans, it thinks of immense expanses of water, it thinks of the immense sea, it thinks of the infinite and of the black ashes of black space, it thinks of vengeance that is naked and devoid of all nuance, it thinks of infinite and black vengeance. It does not think of characters and it neglects the image, for it considers that the image is not of any help. The voice that vociferates neglects the image as violently as it neglects duration, the sense of duration and the idea that time passes. Its intention is to stay as long as possible alongside the humble and terrible animals, alongside humans who are killed and who are burned in ovens, alongside women who are martyrized and who are burned in ovens. Its intention is not to be extinguished regardless of the circumstances that accompany its surge, and even if the world where it vibrates is not adapted to receive it or understand it. The voice that vociferates has the intention of not being extinguished and it has the vocation of not accepting the world as it is or as it has always been. It admits neither the world, nor duration, nor the image, nor extinction. It does not worry about its musicality, it thinks only of its immense and black vengeance, of its naked, immense, black vengeance, devoid of all nuance.

Maria Three-Thirteen, I am speaking to you, she says. Then she is quiet. Deep down, she has no idea of what has passed through her lips and she knows only that she is ashamed of being naked, of being dead, and of having spoken. She feels that she has soot on her arms. She thinks that she must have plunged her hands into the earth and this idea doesn't bother her. At one moment, perhaps she lost her balance, and without realizing it she moved from the crouching position to an even more animal position, closer to the earth. She remains this way for several hours, supposing that one can measure the absence of time in this way. Then she gathers together the motes of energy and will that remain in her and she starts to move very slowly. She moves using all of her limbs to progress. She advances towards nothingness. She no longer breathes. Above her, the sky is a solid block of ink. She is very alone. Not even the least word accompanies her anymore. Her speech is finished, the conference has ended, her audience is no longer even conceivable. She walks with great slowness. Her arms and her legs sink into the dust, then break free of it, then sink into it again. From afar, one would guess a miserable insect dragging itself before its final moments. From close up, too.

I am speaking to you, she thinks again one last time.

Then she continues to walk.

In the end, at least in our post-exotic world, there is also no word. As in the beginning, there is no word. Only the image counts. The voices are quiet and only the image counts. Whether it is extinguished or not, whether it means something of not, in the end, and when I say the end it's really the end, only the image counts.

TOMORROW WILL HAVE BEEN A LOVELY SUNDAY

Nikita Kouriline wasn't called to be a writer; he didn't have a great aptitude for it, and this status as marginal, as an inferior and excluded creature, had no reason to tempt him, but in the end he became one, he had become one for better or worse at his birth on an unpaved street in Iemerovo, south of Moscow, on June 27, 1938. His grandmother claimed he was born on a Sunday.

It was a Sunday, a lovely Sunday, she said, it was, yes, nonetheless, a lovely Sunday. The bells were ringing. Your mother was screaming, legs spread above her blood, she was emptying herself, she was dying, the bells were ringing at full peal, it was a warm June day, through the window we saw the birches shimmering as though each of their leaves had been replaced by a little mirror. For her as for all of us, it should have been a superb Sunday, but she was dying. The midwife had lost her calm. She reassured your mother despite the blood, but increasingly, her voice would skid and she, too, cried out. You hadn't yet completely come out, the cord was strangling you, the bells were ringing at full peal, I opened the window to try to get rid of the smells of butchery and death that were escaping from your mother's body, for don't believe, Nikita, that the smells of childbirth are agreeable or at least neutral, no, on the contrary, they're unbearable. The chiming of the bells rushed even more strongly into the room, I started shouting over the noise, and almost immediately I closed the window again, and when I turned around, you had finally emerged, the cord had stopped choking you and your mother was dead.

Kouriline had heard this story many times, with variations, since his grandmother tended towards epic exaggeration and gossip, and now, when he recited it to himself, he no longer felt the emotion or embarrassment that he had always felt during his childhood. The trauma had been terrible when, still very young, he had learned that his arrival in the world had accompanied and perhaps provoked the death of his mother. Forty-five years later, when he figured he had already reached the edge beyond which there is nothing, besides perhaps an inevitable degradation along the road leading to the cemetery, his feeling of guilt remained. He had succeeded in stuffing it beneath other discomforts and other bad memories, but deep down, the wound was impossible to close. Little by little, nonetheless, the story that his grandmother told had drifted towards something confusedly literary, composed of a succession of powerful but artificial images, as though it were a cinematographic sequence whose content had long ago been exhausted, too often rehashed to awaken the old suffering. His grandmother was no longer there to deftly stir up what terrified him or caused him pain. In this film that he watched and re-watched, the streaming savagery, the howls, the noisy hysteria, the racket of the bells, had taken on such exaggerated colors that the tragic was no longer credible. Kouriline felt less concerned and he even began to permit himself, in the last few years, to watch with a shrug of his shoulders.

Often, with closed eyes, he listened again to his grandmother's warm voice, the voice of an actress, and his thinking towards her softened. He admired her gift for storytelling and he remembered the first time that he had questioned the veracity of the details and the twists that made the scene so vivid and so impressive. It had taken him a while to admit that his grandmother was prone to literary inventions, but one day, when he was already a shamefaced and gloomy teenager, permanently dismayed at owing his existence to a crime, he had a revelation: the bells. No bells could have rung in Iemerovo on June 27, 1938, whether it was a Sunday or any other day. At that time, the Orthodox churches were in a delicate state with the regime, to say the least. The anti-religious battle wasn't as fierce or enthusiastic as it had been in the twenties, but it still existed, and the clergy avoided officiating in broad daylight. One could still find priests with darting eyes, on high alert and terrorized by their daily routine of semi-clandestinity, and services were still taking place, but the bells were silent. It's impossible, he had said to his grandmother. The bells were silent back then.

What do you mean, impossible? My grandmother had replied angrily. There was a bell tower less than one hundred meters from the house, I swear to you, I remember it as though it were yesterday. The sky was clear, it was a marvelous Sunday, a marvelous June Sunday. I opened the windows because the bedroom was stifling. Your mother had not stopped groaning since the middle of the night. Dawn was painful. The bedroom smelled bad, I couldn't stand to keep breathing these emanations of sweat, of dilated organs, and of dirty laundry, the midwife's hair reeked, her veterinary apron was impeccable but her dress must have served her all week, she got dressed quickly to come, without changing, with whatever she had on hand, with her already tired clothing, you know how sensitive I am to odors, your mother much less so, but you inherited it, you too, Nikita, you can't stand unpleasant odors, we are alike, neither of us can stand it. And so I went towards the windows and I opened them, but the midwife forbade it, she was part of that school of obstetrics that thinks the delivery should unfold in a place that's nearly airtight and devoid of witnesses, moreover she would have liked me to leave but I refused to do so, I firmly refused, first because Galia was my daughter and also because this midwife was upsetting me, an incapable woman who was certified but who I suspected was no good, incompetent, and perhaps had inroads with the agencies where people denounced their neighbors and everyone else. I closed the casement and at that moment the bells began to ring for the first time, but it was still early. I have no idea what time it was. For a long time after that it was again as though the room was watertight, separated from everything, then you began to come out. The crowning of your bare, purplish skull was so dreadful that I couldn't bear seeing it for more than a few seconds, and then the hemorrhaging was so violent that I thought I would vomit. While the midwife was struggling, I went and leaned against the window. Your mother refused to let anyone take her hand, she refused all assistance, she refused my presence, she refused everything, she did nothing but wail like an animal led to slaughter, whose throat someone has clumsily started to slit and failed. I had the hardest time seeing her as my daughter rather than an obscene animal in repulsive agony. She no longer had a command of language, she no longer addressed herself to anyone, she let loose pitiful howls that wouldn't differentiate her from a sheep or a cow under the butcher's knife. Pardon me, Nikita, for telling you these things in such a brutal way, but it's true, I could no longer manage to see her as someone human, as someone with whom I had blood ties, as someone who, in better moments, could have turned towards me and shown me that she was my daughter. I felt nothing in particular towards her, aside from exasperation, and even a vague aversion. I never had a maternal instinct, I had never been pleased to have a daughter, feeling genetically responsible for a daughter revolted me. You see, Nikita, I hide nothing from you. I never wanted to pass for someone exemplary. But anyway. I know that it was Sunday because of the bells. Another day, there would have been no noise outside, or only the sound of a truck passing along the road, or a few echoes of conversation. Not much noise, in any case; it was a village, and a rather deserted village at that. And there, there were the bells. I couldn't have invented that, obviously. I assure you, Nikita, I couldn't have invented that. I remember that morning as though it were yesterday. It was June 27, 1938, south of Moscow, and I assure you that it was a Sunday. The bells were ringing, the sun was shining, it was a lovely Sunday. It was the day of your birth, a lovely Sunday. It could have turned out well, when you think about it.

Nikita Kouriline's grandmother's voice was velvety and deep. He had spent his childhood listening to her, obeying her, and believing what she said. They had lived together, his grandmother and he, they had lived in Iemerovo, then, when the Germans approached Moscow, they had emigrated towards the forgotten towns deep in the Urals. Kulgulinko, Baikaziorovo, Askariovo. From time to time, maybe once or twice a year, she told him the story of his birth, she started again from the beginning, from this atrocious departure. It's in case you haven't grasped the worth of a human life, she would say. The bells were ringing at full peal, she would insist. Which bells? asked Nikita Kouriline. He was eight years old, he was still too young to doubt her story, but somehow, this detail already grated on him. He rubbed his nose with the back of a mitten to get the blood flowing, so that the extremity attacked by frost didn't lose contact with life, didn't fall off. The bells, explained the grandmother to the little boy. The counterrevolutionaries' bells, the clergy's bells, the Orthodox reactionaries' bells, the anti-Soviets' bells, the Trotskyists' bells, the bells of the spies from Austria, Germany, Japan, the English. They rang at full peal. We heard nothing but them. Even your mother had to bray more loudly to make herself heard. The midwife asked her to tone down her wailing. She tried to convince her that all women had gone through it before her. Then the hemorrhaging started, the hemorrhaging was torrential, and the midwife stopped reproaching your mother. The bells played no role in the story. The bells ... insisted the little boy. Never in my life have I heard them chime, never have I heard a Sunday with bells. That's normal, commented Nikita Kouriline's grandmother. You live in another era. In '38, they still used to ring. I remember all that as though it were yesterday. They rang at full peal. It was south of Moscow, next to Butovo, in Iemerovo, Tchernogradskaya Street. Perhaps there was an exception in this place, I can't say. But they were chiming. There was a bell tower not far from the house and it was ringing at full peal. It made the birth even more monstrous. The first sounds that you heard were your mother's groans, and the midwife's panic as she pretended not to be panicked, and the bells. You don't remember, of course, my poor boy, but that's what it was. That's how it was.

Kouriline didn't feel the need to write down fables or unburden himself on the world in which he had landed in order to live, nor the desire to entrust to paper his moods and his disappointments, nor the worry of teaching a lesson to others. He had nothing writerly in him, and moreover the level of education that he had reached by the age of about twenty wouldn't have helped him in the slightest had he wanted to give himself over to the disingenuous and upstart activities that are typically grouped under the pompous term of literature. He had no degree, he knew how to wire electric sockets, repair washing machines and tractor motors, but he preferred not to specialize, and he went from one precarious job to another, sometimes a caretaker, sometimes a day laborer, sometimes a janitor or a server in factory cafeterias, or again as a handyman in obscure administrations. His grandmother was now dead, he had no family, and, on the sentimental and sexual front, nothing really notable had ever happened to him, girls having always considered him a good-for-nothing. He slept without being able to remember his dreams, he didn't read books, the knowledge he had gained at school unraveled, the intellectual poverty and the monotony of his day-to-day life hollowed out an emptiness in him that he didn't rush to fill, and of which he was not ashamed, for he was surrounded by people who, like him, knew that their existence was worth nothing, was leading to nothing, aside from the grave, and who, once that fact was established, couldn't care less.

One evening when he happened on an old perpetual calendar, he searched, as everyone always does, to verify which day of the week corresponded with his date of birth. It was a Sunday that could have been marvelous, his grandmother had said. It took him less than a minute to discover that June 27, 1938 had been a Monday. This discovery petrified him. He couldn't manage to conceive that, on this detail as well, his grandmother had lied. He had long called into question the bells' racket, and even the amount of blood that his mother had spilled, but he had never dreamed of objecting to this Sunday business. Once he had emerged from the state of turmoil that this new revelation had plunged him into, he called his grandmother's story to mind. Iemerovo, Butovo, the forest of Drojjino, the ambience of a Russian village, poplars, birches, pines, bells that raged, the beauty of a June day, the closed windows, opened and noisily closed again, the calm outside and the tragedy within, the smell of blood, a baby who was presenting badly, a baby who slipped from one world to the other in the midst of a sinister flow and who struggled, purplish and deadly, who insisted on surviving whatever the cost, who chose, as the first link in the chain of its existence, to leave behind a sea of blood and a cadaver.

Everyone was covered with sweat, his grandmother said. Births are all alike, it's good form to pretend that they're accompanied by a notion of happiness, and that the pain of contractions is more than compensated for by the tranquil joy of the delivery and by the appearance of the newborn. But it's often quite false. The suffering is indescribable, the anguish that precedes the birth is crushing, labor is nothing but a succession of fears and cramps. And let me tell you, Nikita. It's also a moment when you're alarmed at being so female, so animal. You feel the weight of all animality for tens of millions of years and the weight is too heavy, it crushes you. Of the whole process, the long expulsion of the baby from your entrails is the worst.

Other females move around you, they touch you, they tear you apart, they talk to you, and you sense in the depths of their voices that they are fundamentally disgusted by your body, by your lower body, by your way of enduring this calving as though it were a disease, a sharp crisis point in a painful disease. They reassure you, they say stupid, supposedly reassuring things, but in the depths of their voices you discern a negative judgment of you, they think you could be braver, that you're reacting badly to suffering, that you aren't trying hard enough, that you're just mediocre in your role of happy mother. I suppose that Galia was haunted by all that and that her feelings of shame and grief mixed with her terrible pain, and perhaps because of that she didn't feel herself die. I don't know. I wished it intensely in that moment and I continue to wish with all my strength that that was the case. I didn't touch her, I didn't tear her apart like the midwife did, I was there, in the bedroom, more as a useless witness than as someone who could provide assistance. I glanced from time to time at what was happening and I saw the overflowing blood. The air in the room was unbreathable. Everyone was covered with sweat. Your mother was dripping, the sweat was getting lost amidst all the various liquids that were emptying from her. The midwife leaned over, clearly facing complications that she didn't know how to treat, and the smell of her dirty sweat spread all around her, forcing me to stay close to the window rather than close to the bed. I was very damp myself, I couldn't take the heat or nervousness anymore, I couldn't take this powerlessness, this anger at destiny, I couldn't take being faced with birth and faced with death. I couldn't breathe anymore. When I opened the window, the midwife ordered me to close it again. The bells rang obsessively. They wouldn't stop. When I think of it, of everything in those terrible hours, the carillon was the most unbearable. Yes, it was unbearable. Exactly, yes. Unbearable.

The idea of having been misled for forty-five years on such decisive elements of his existence revived the feelings of doubt, of disgust, and of guilt that he had thought covered over and even attenuated by time, but, in parallel, gave him the impression that he could now take over the story, that he could insert himself into it without counting any longer on an intermediate voice. He had come to understand that his birth could also be reported using words and even details that belonged to him, that his birth was a fiction that from now on would depend entirely on him. His grandmother, his mother, the midwife, the bells, the odors, the window, the blood, the newborn who was presenting badly, everything could be combined differently, in the form of a different story that would obey him and that perhaps, finally, would calm him.

That is how, in 1983, Nikita Kouriline was struck by the need to write. He's not dreaming of a book, he's not dreaming of anything in particular, he only knows that he must start again at zero with his birth and that that means putting down on paper the exact unfolding, point by point, of the event that he holds dear. Since he does not have the gift of imagination, he sets off to research other elements than those the perpetual calendar has provided. His investigation has no foundation, he conducts it with no method, searching high and low and counting on chance. Several times during the course of these difficult months, he hangs around the places that his grandmother evoked, Iemerovo, the woods of Drojjino, Butovo, Bobrovo. He laboriously researches what happened on June 27, 1938, he doesn't find anything special, and then, suddenly, he learns that the place had been chosen by the NKVD to shoot twenty thousand people during the purges. These are difficult months, because he is depressed, jobless again, very lonely, and because the weather is grey and foreboding. With a bad conscience, he wanders in the alleys that have now been traced between the pines and birches of Drojjino, he inhales the scent of the bark, the humid thickets, he walks without haste and without pleasure on the dead leaves, on the rotten needles, in the mud. His native village has been disfigured by the development of a residential zone, nobody has ever heard of Tchernogradskaya Street, none of the elderly people remember his grandmother. The house of his birth no longer exists, none of the elderly people recall ever having caught wind of the existence of an NKVD execution center, as for the youths, they openly mock him and turn their backs on him, or give him fictitious directions. There is nothing to promote the reconstruction of his memories. Now he roams near the Butovo polygon where almost nothing is left. Under his feet are mass graves and thousands of dead people.

Under the mushrooms, under the mediocre light of autumn, under the rain. There are dead people. There are thousands of people who have been killed.

For a moment, he tries to write. Something compels him to do it. But he can't seem to organize his story and, try as he might, he ends up with a series of unbalanced sentences, jumbles of words that don't tell the story of his birth, nor of the death of his mother, nor of the massacre that was happening on the other side of Drojjino forest. All his editing attempts are aborted after half a page. This first horrifying chapter of his existence has never brought him anything but torment and shame, which are now compounded by the feeling of his incompetence as a writer. He loses patience, for he lets himself be overcome by the idea that he has a literary obligation to accomplish. His story has a title he's rather proud of, *Story of a Sunday that was a Monday*, but what comes next is missing. He works on it for weeks, he accumulates stubs that he abandons after having crossed them out completely. He has just moved into a basement, in the entrance of a furniture factory that hired him and where he provides security from nightfall to early morning.

He has no friends, and moreover, his literary enterprise has cut him off from the outside world. Nonetheless, the two factory caretakers, who watch over the entrances and exits during the day, are friendly with him. One of them, Daaz Doguiwlo, once had trouble with the police, which he refuses to talk about. The other, Utchur Tenderekov, has a psychiatric history. It's with these two that Kouriline converses about his poetic project. He talks to them above all about his inability to tell on paper what he can more or less manage to say. He also summarizes the affair for them. He speaks of Butovo, of Sunday, of Monday, of his grandmother, of the bestial horror of the birth. He has trouble recognizing aloud that his mother died the minute he was born, so he doesn't say it. But he gives the detail of the bells, he repeats the date. With the caretakers, he shares sweet wine, beer, vodka.

The man who had trouble with the police speculates about the archives of the NKVD, about the lists of names that appear in dossiers that haven't been destroyed, about the lists enumerating those shot between 1937 and 1938, about the sheets of paper where the men of Iejov inscribed the names of the condemned from the Butovo polygon, about the sheet dated June 27. The man who had spent time in insane asylums, Utchur Tenderekov, claims that he already has one of these papers. He has seen it in his dream, he knows where it is, he's waiting for a favorable occasion to see it again, to take it and bring it back to Nikita Kouriline. They've had a lot to drink. Outside, it's dark, the rain and the wind slam against the windowpanes. Utchur Tenderekov climbs on a chair and waves his arms so that the dream will come back to him even now. He is unhinged. He's a former mental patient and it seems that he's falling into a relapse. He gesticulates, he explains that he is ordering forces to enter him, that he is ordering his memory to reconstitute everything, that he is ordering the executed to shout their names to him, and, from time to time, he wavers and he sobs. If he wasn't lit so starkly by the bare light bulb, you might think he was possessed, that he had returned to his native Altai and that he was giving himself over to a séance of shamanic invocation. Then he gives names, he recites one after another the records of the men whom the NKVD assassinated. He reads them out loud as though he had them before his eyes.

Worn out, by the alcohol as much as by the lugubrious invocation of the dead, Daaz Doguiwlo and Nikita Kouriline listen to what does indeed sound like a list, the beginning of an interminable list.

"Abrachine, Stepan Fyodorovitch! … Born in 1884, Obiltsevo hamlet, Detchinskiy district, Moscow region! … Russian, elementary education, no party! … Reinforced concrete factory, in charge of heating, Moscow address, Fifth Avenue Donskoy, house number 25! … Arrested April 12, 1938, judged June 3, 1938 by a troika of the Moscow OUNKVD, charge: counterrevolutionary agitation! … Shot June 27, 1938, place of burial: Butovo! Alekseyev, Artiom Mikhailovitch! … Born in 1894, Dermanovka village, Bazarskiy district, Kiev region, Russian! … Elementary education, no party! … Agricultural laborer in possession of a horse, living in the village of Kotlyakovo, Lenininskiy district, Moscow region! … Arrested April 4, 1938, judged June 3 by a troika of the Moscow OUNKVD! …

Grounds of charge: counterrevolutionary agitation, calumnious declarations on the party's politics and on Soviet power! ... Shot June 27, 1938, place of burial: Butovo! ... Bakhatov Vasilii Vasilievitch! ... Born in 1890 in the village of Degtianskoye, Kozlovskiy district, province of Tambov! ... Russian! ... Elementary education! ... No party, enrolled in the Udarnik artel, independent cart driver! ... Resides in Moscow, Vladimirskiy quarter, barracks No. 1, arrested March 26, 1938! Judged June 3, 1938 by a troika of the regional OUNKVD, for counterrevolutionary agitation among the workers in his lodging and terrorist attitudes towards the party director! ... Shot! ... June 27, 1938! ... Buried in Butovo! ... Gaidar Afanasy Fyodorovich, born in 1872! ... Born in the village of Grinki, Semyonovskiy district, Kharkov region, Ukrainian! Elementary education, no party, works on construction of the metro as a laborer in pit No. 57! ... Address: Moscow, Lefortovskiy rampart, No. 12, lodging of Metrostroy workers, barracks No. 3! ... Arrest January 21, 1938! Judged June 3, 1938, by a troika based within the regional OUNKVD, on the accusation of anti-Soviet agitation! ... Anti-Soviet agitation and terrorist intentions! ... Shot June 27, 1938! ... Buried in Butovo!

Utchur Tenderekov's inspiration dies out after fifteen minutes. He manages to get down from his chair without falling, then collapses at the feet of the other two. They don't know if he's blitzed because of the vodka or because the forces that he invoked have abruptly left him. He breathes and groans in a disconcerting manner, then he starts to snore. It'll be okay, Daaz Doguiwlo grumbles vaguely. He'll recover and it'll be okay. As for Daaz Doguiwlo, he no longer resists the need to sleep. Kouriline abandons them in the bright, stinking, sordid little room, and leaves to take up his surveillance duties. He checks the locks on the gates, the locks on the warehouses, the workshops, he circles the entrance area, he walks along the echoing tunnels. The night is dense, the rain noisy. The workshops emit powerful perfumes of wood, oil, and varnish. Kouriline leans against the doors, he zigzags along his round route, he talks to himself. He murmurs names that continue those that Utchur Tenderekov trumpeted an hour earlier. He is extremely troubled, extremely sad, and he is intoxicated. He leans against a grate, face turned towards the rain, jacket open to the wind and the nocturnal darkness. He again says names, minimalist biographical elements, dates of arrest. His voice is a wine-soaked lament; it's also a reproach launched into the night. It doesn't carry far, four or five meters at the very most. Wind and fatigue cancel them out immediately. But it addresses an invisible public, invisible clouds, obscure trickles born in the dark skies, it addresses the dead.

When morning comes, Kouriline wakes up. Unconscious, in the middle of the night, he dragged himself beneath a shelter. His limbs and torso are frozen, his clothes are still soaked. Hands clenching a bit of wood, a fallen branch from a pine tree rounded in the shape of a bowling pin, he regains contact with the world. He shivers and heads towards his basement. The first shift is already hard at work, the sound of the saw starting up resonates from the workshops. Kouriline goes down the stairs and pushes the door that leads to his minuscule apartment. The lamp is still on, but nobody is there anymore, his drinking buddies must have gotten back to their work posts in one way or another and unchained the gates for deliveries, opened the main entrance. In the room where Kouriline lives, the odors of drunks are strong. He flips open the basement window to get fresh air, he tidies up, aligns the bottles in one corner, cleans the floor. He washes, shaves, he changes his underwear, then he lies down in his unmade bed that smells of piss, then he gets up again. He knows that he won't be able to sleep and the thought occurs to him that he will never sleep well again, at least until his death, until he rejoins those who were shot the day of his birth, the minute of his birth, the precise moment when he fought to disobey the death of his mother and to escape the cord that was strangling him, to escape at any cost that initial and terminal apnea. He takes a pencil and he tries again to pour out on the paper all that fills his head, but after two illiterate lines, he cuts himself off. On the table, the pin resembles an illegible totem. It's neither a pin, nor an identifiable article of furniture, nor a crude representation of the divine or the human. It's just a bit of wood abandoned by the carpenters after a disappointing minute of work on the lathe.

It's only a bit of wood, but Kouriline sets aside his useless writing paraphernalia and talks to it.

"Abrachine, Stepane Fyodorovich, you were afraid. You were afraid after your arrest, while they interrogated you, while they tried to make you say counterrevolutionary idiocies, during all those interminable weeks of April, May, and June. You didn't understand anything, you kept thinking that everything would turn out okay, you knew, deep down, that they couldn't imprison you for nothing, that they weren't going to send you to the camps on charges fabricated out of thin air. They had smashed your face, your mouth was bleeding, you couldn't sleep, you were afraid. I was keeping a low profile during that time, too. You were afraid, but you still had a bit of hope. You didn't speak to the other detainees. Abrachine, during that period, I too was afraid. Nobody was there to listen to me, and, deep down, I knew well that I wasn't going to escape unscathed from where I was, that I was going to emerge into poor conditions. Now, Abrachine, I'm speaking to you. We're together. Try not to be afraid anymore. We had a hope in common, both of us, but it didn't turn out well. Together, let's try to talk about all that. I'm listening."

With this speech to the bit of wood, that morning Kouriline launched the scansion of his unique but considerable body of work, which would make him into one of the most unrecognized writers of his century, and, if one refers to a precise literary periodization, undoubtedly the most unknown writer of the perestroika, the one who clearly left the fewest traces in the world of idle word.

Kouriline doesn't write. He refuses to inscribe what he has to say in ink.

What he has to say, he says it.

His novel had several titles, *Story of a Sunday that Was a Monday, Sunday Didn't Exist that Day, A Monday of Blood,* but in the end Kouriline chose *Tomorrow Will Have Been a Lovely Sunday* and didn't change it again, perhaps because he realized that the title no longer had the least importance for him.

The important thing was for him to tirelessly continue his work, and to devote his existence to it.

Kouriline's novel consists of several parts that are not successive, but rather constantly intertwine and weave a strong fabric, brutal and indestructible, that can at any moment be reinforced by new supports. The author doesn't worry about the musical ordering of the ensemble of his multiple narrative compositions, because he knows that they hold together tremendously among themselves, that they cannot be dissociated and that nothing will undo them as long as he is alive to pronounce them. The essential parts of Kouriline's novel are the following: list of the dead, particular circumstances of their arrests, of their passage before the troika of NKVD magistrates, particular circumstances of their deaths; detailed description of the June 27 birth; reflections on the political positions of the baby's grandmother, on the impossibility for her of recognizing that the echoes that filled the air that day weren't the vibrations of bells, but an interminable succession of volleys emanating from an execution squad; bleak autobiography of Kouriline; drunken monologues, combining anecdotal and recurrent subjects, like the problems of heat supply, the poor quality of television, the absence of basic courtesy in stores; imaginary biographies of the executed.

Kouriline brings together rags, bits of iron or bits of wood, occasionally dolls, to whom he attributes an identity. He considers them simultaneously as an audience and as a collection of characters. He is careful never to bump against his interlocutors, and he speaks to each of them in an affectionate, brotherly voice, with the will to create a welcoming universe where he can set down his desolation without emphasizing himself too much. He doesn't want the dead to feel responsible for his unhappiness. He doesn't complain, and when he strikes a plaintive tone, it's to accompany the discourses that he lends to the victims in their cells, in the solitude that precedes their execution, during the moments when nearby the rifle shots are audible, robbing them of all hope.

He creates a sort of collection of debris gathered from the factory's trash dump, then from the streets, later, when he loses his job as night watchman and wanders with a bag on his shoulder containing all of his riches, and later still, when he moves into a dilapidated little house, half burned down, that is being lent to him in exchange for a rather roughly defined surveillance assignment for the construction site of an apartment building that makes no progress, that the snow covers, where the wind blows day and night, where nobody ever makes an appearance, not an engineer, nor an architect, nor a businessman, nor a workman tasked with maintenance. The construction site is reduced to a few stacks of girders, already badly rusted, and an immense inhospitable terrain. From time to time, Kouriline walks around the site, then returns to shiver near his stove in the burned-down house. Surrounding him are several circles of debris and it's to them that he dedicates the new little chapters of his book, it's before them that he recites again and again the numerous sequences already completed, and that his semi-illiterate memory restores slowly but without a hitch, without a single omission, without parasitic embellishments.

He faces his audience and he speaks his work.

The names of the executed he calls them to himself like Utchur Tenderekov called them, during that famous night of drinking. He calls them to himself and they come to him. Utchur Tenderekov cannot be found. He disappeared, and, according to Daaz Doguiwlo, his family intervened to get him admitted to a psychiatric establishment. Kouriline tried to find out which establishment, he planned to visit him and take advantage of his occult knowledge to complete the list that he needed for his novel, but Daaz Doguiwlo had no clues, no address, and the last time Kouriline went to see him at the furniture factory, they told him that the watchman had been fired like him for serious misconduct, which is to say for state of intoxication while on the clock. So Kouriline no longer has any reliable source that would allow him to construct his novel on the real, and he must fall back on his own inspiration. He drinks, he climbs on a chair under the lamp with no lampshade, he gesticulates, as though heavily dancing on the spot, and the names of the June 27 victims come to him.

"Dedyonok," he calls, "Dedyonok Mikhail Ermolayevich! ... Belarusian, no party! ... Born in 1902 in Troyanovo, Krupki district, Belarus! ... Illiterate, unskilled workman in the Stankolit factory! ... Living in Moscow, 20, Skladochnaya Street, barracks 10, room 11, arrested March 16, 1938! ... Judged June 3, 1938 by a troika of the regional OUNKVD of Moscow, charged with counterrevolutionary agitation among the workers of the Stankolit factory, with negative commentary and calumny on life in the USSR, with insults towards the Party directors and Soviet power! ... Shot June 27, 1938! ..."

Sometimes, in moving his arms above his head, he touches the lamp. The light bulb burns him. He pulls back his hand, grumbling, and continues.

"Dimitrov," he goes on, "Nikolai Petrovich! ... Born in 1902 in Tergokeni, Bacau, Romania! ... Jew! ... No party, college education interrupted! . . . Employed as typesetter No. 21, resides in Moscow, at 23 First Meshchanskaya Street, apartment 43, arrested March 3, 1938! ... Judged May 29 by an NKVD commission for espionage on behalf of Romanian intelligence! ... Shot June 27, 1938, thrown into a mass grave in Butovo! ..."

He doesn't always stay planted on the chair. He gets down from it, he walks around the main room of the house, he moves slowly in all directions, shrugging his shoulders, tapping his feet on the parquet floor that escaped the fire, but from which a black powder that no broom eliminates sometimes rises. He takes in his hands the metal debris, the shards of wood to which he has given names, the handfuls of cloth that listen to him. He takes them in his hands, murmuring, and he puts them back into place. This is a break that he is giving them, so that the tension associated with the enunciation of crimes will be somewhat attenuated. It's an amicable greeting, a catastrophic mark of affection. Next he will clear his throat with a swallow of wine. Then he climbs back on the chair and takes up his novel again.

"Kuzmichev, Stepan Andreyevich!..." he sobs. "Born in 1881 in the village of Polyanka, Chern district, Tula province! Russian, elementary education, no party! ... Caretaker in a pedagogical institute, lives in Moscow, 64 Usievicha Street, apartment No. 6, arrested March 28, 1938, condemned June 3, 1938 by a troika of the regional OUNKVD of Moscow! ... Accusation: counterrevolutionary agitation alongside teachers and neighbors in his apartment building, systematic anti-Soviet calumnies and propaganda, shot! ... Shot June 27, 1938 in the Butovo polygon! ... Buried in Butovo! ..."

It can also happen that he undertakes a discussion with his grandmother about her obstinacy in claiming to have heard bells ring, when in reality she was hearing rifle shots that reverberated between the Butovo polygon's walls, in the wasteland that adjoined the NKVD barracks. He is convinced now that his grandmother unconsciously transformed her memories. She didn't want to evoke the massacre in front of him, nor did she want to conserve it in her memory. There were too many deaths and there was too much blood that day, and the only way to confront the tragedy was to minimize it and to believe that, in spite of everything, in spite of everything, it could have been a beautiful day, a lovely Sunday or a lovely Monday in June. But Kouriline isn't satisfied with this fairly mechanical explanation of oblivion. He also reflects on his grandmother's attitude with regard to the crime. It's one of the important developments of his novel.

His grandmother was an enthusiast of the communist party, as was he, Kouriline, for that matter, an enthusiast without party affiliation but convinced that the chosen path was historically good, a woman profoundly sure that collectivism and egalitarianism opened a scintillating perspective in the historical chaos that humans and the assimilated traversed; his grandmother, like him, Kouriline, was an inalienable supporter of the Soviet system, was sensitive to Leninism and benevolent towards the person and the theory no matter what happened, and, like him, she didn't imagine for a moment that she could side with the enemies of the USSR, she didn't consent for a moment to letting her voice mix with the barking of the fascists and capitalists who were besieging the socialist party, she knew full well that the socialism under construction, that real socialism, was an appalling and non-Marxist reality, but, if she bitterly critiqued the conditions of her daily life, she refused to draw the conclusion that the system had completely failed, that the system was fundamentally bad and that the future of the system was its crumbling. Kouriline shared her views during the time that she could take the floor before him, and then, when she was no longer anything but a memory and a model, he continued to think like her. He is forty-five years old, forty-six years old, forty-seven years old, the strange years of glasnost and perestroika arrive, but he continues to think like her.

When he speaks to his grandmother, he tries to make her say that she tolerated the executions. She avoids taking a position, she avoids the subject. He insists. She states that at that time it was necessary to ferociously neutralize internal enemies, saboteurs, and spies. He asks her if she had the chance to denounce one or two of them. She responds that she never denounced anyone, but that, if she had had to do it, she would have carried out her obligation as a Soviet. He asks her if she was sure that the proletarians and the poor people who had been arrested, judged in an expedited fashion, and executed were really counterrevolutionary scoundrels. She sighs, she says that she wasn't sure, but that the NKVD was there to determine it, and that at that time there was no reason to condemn innocent people.

He, Kouriline, also sighs.

He takes as witnesses the bits of wood, the metallic spindles coarsely dressed up in cloths so that they resemble dolls, the twists and the balls of fabric. None are anonymous any longer. He knows every one.

He caresses these improbable ruins one after another. Each one has an identity.

"Kuzmine," he says in a soft voice. "Ivanov, Leksakov, Lebedev, Matveyev, Podzorov! … Prokopenko, Svirichev, Skorynine! … Uly-anov! … Fyodorov! …"

He holds long, murmuring conversations with them, which constitute part of his novel but that sometimes he prefers not to conserve, and that are therefore not included when he recites from the beginning the vast narrative that he has undertaken. He has doubts, actually, about what he can write and not write. He confides in the executed, he devotes his writing time to them, he soothes them, and he expresses all his affection to them, but some nights, he ventures into their files and he wonders whether, all things considered, they might not in fact be active enemies of the society that we are building, that we are trying to build, that we are sacrificing ourselves day and night to build. He says "we" in thinking of his grandmother and of the population that didn't really have anything to do with the men of Iejov, and also in thinking of those whom the men of Iejov beat and tortured in order to make them confess nonsense. He says "we" in thinking of himself, in putting himself in the place that he would have occupied had he been an adult at the time. He asks them that, and the others don't respond to him. Those pages are the most muddled and most arduous of *Tomorrow Will Have Been a Lovely Sunday*. Once spoken, they are the most muddled and the most arduous. While Kouriline gives the floor to the condemned, to those who wait in their overcrowded cell or who walk towards the soldiers, who approach the pit that was dug for them during the night, while he tries to see the events again through the eyes of his grandmother, in turn he contrives, like her, not to believe in the executions.

At one point, he says, I opened the window. The midwife was busy with your mother, and, over her shoulder, without looking at me, she ordered me to close it again. I protested and didn't obey right away. The stinking heat in the room was unbearable. I was suffocating, I suppose Galia was suffocating, too. I couldn't take it anymore, watching this awful collapse of her body, I was floored by the intuition that was sharpening in me and that was telling me with more and more certainty that my daughter was going to die, that Galia was going to die very soon, without consolation and without solace. Outside, the June sky shone, the birches trembled beneath the light and beneath the warmth. There were regular sounds, violent echoes that were rolling from beyond the trees.

There were regular sounds, violent echoes that were rolling from beyond the trees.

I closed the window again.

For several years, Nikita Kouriline's novel evolves little. The author consolidates the prison monologue passages, adds a few names of characters standing on the ground of Butovo, hearing the volleys from very near, waiting to go and place themselves before the soldiers. Solovyev, Russian, illiterate, longshoreman, counterrevolutionary agitation and insurrectionist attitudes. Pimenov, Russian, illiterate, night watchman, hostile disposition towards the Soviet power. Skamper, Austrian, illiterate, locksmith, espionage for the benefit of Austria. Streltsov, Russian, illiterate, workman, espionage, transmission of secret facts to a Japanese intelligence agency. Stukoline, Russian, illiterate, shopkeeper, counterrevolutionary activities among the residents of his apartment building. Ulchine, Russian, illiterate, workman in a kolkhoz, counterrevolutionary agitation among his co-detainees.

In the various lodgings where Kouriline lives, and that bear witness to his professional instability, Kouriline establishes his novel with care and patiently says it again, taking his time and without much variation. He tends to his relationships with those condemned to death. The bits of iron and the wooden debris have been provided with labels, ribbons, and wisps of colored wool that humanize them more and more and individualize them. He recognizes them at first glance and he talks to them, choosing his words so that the literary language won't bewilder them, so that they will find themselves together without passing through the nauseous intermediary of official poetry. When he has the chance, he tells them of his birth that was their terrible end. He cautiously mixes his mother's blood with their own blood. It sometimes happens that he tries to justify his grandmother's confusions while speaking with them, but he reserves that chapter's developments for private conversations with her.

His voice is hoarse, and often his sadness is so great that he ceases to speak, leaving the last pages fallow.

June 27, 1988, he is fifty years old. It's a Monday.

He gathers his characters around him, on the ground that he has neither swept nor washed for three weeks, on the malodorous mattress where he has just spent a bad night, on the table full of crumbs and stains of undrinkable wines, on the two wobbly chairs that a neighbor lent him when he moved into this tiny place. He speaks again to his characters. They are all dead. Including the midwife, his grandmother, his mother, and himself, there are one hundred and forty-five, which automatically propels him among the great polyphonic writers of the last years of the USSR. Then, he grabs an electric wire that he collected from a construction site the night before. And then, he hangs himself.

ALBERT-BIROT, PIERRE,
The First Book of Grabinoulor.

BELLETTO, RENÉ,
Dying.

BREBEL, SEBASTIEN,
Villa Bunker ,

BUTOR, MICHEL, *Degrees,*
Mobile,
Portrait of the Artist as a Young Ape.

CÉLINE, LOUIS-FERDINAND,
Castle to Castle,
Conversations with Professor Y
London Bridge, Normance,
North, Rigadoon.

CERF, MURIEL,
Street Girl.

CHAIX, MARIE,
The Laurels of Lake Constance,
Silences, or a Woman's Life,
The Summer of the Elder Tree.

CHAWAF, CHANTAL,
Redemption.

CHEVILLARD, ERIC,
Demolishing Nisard .

CHOLODENKO, MARC,
Mordechai Schamz.

CREVEL, RENÉ,
Putting My Foot In It.

ECHENOZ, JEAN,
Chopin's Move.

ERNAUX, ANNIE,
Cleaned Out.

FLAUBERT, GUSTAVE,
Bouvard and Pécuchet.

GAVARRY, GÉRARD,
Hoppla!,
Making a Novel.

GILSON, ETIENNE,
The Arts of the Beautiful,
Forms and Substances in the Arts.

GRAINVILLE, PATRICK,
The Cave of Heaven.

JOUET, JACQUES,
My Beautiful Bus,

Mountain R,
Savage,
Upstaged.

JULIET, CHARLES,
Conversations with Samuel Beckett and Bram
van Velde .

KLOSSOWSKI, PIERRE,
Roberte Ce Soir: And the Revocation of the Edict
of Nantes.

LAURRENT, ERIC,
Do Not Touch.

LE TELLIER, HERVÉ,
The Sextine Chapel,
A Thousand Pearls (for a Thousand Pennies).

LEDUC, VIOLETTE,
La Bâtarde.

LEVÉ, EDOUARD,
Autoportrait,
Suicide.

LOZEREC'H, BRIGITTE,
Sisters.

MONTALBETTI, CHRISTINE,
The Origin of Man,
Western.

NAVARRE, YVES,
Our Share of Time,
Sweet Tooth.

OLLIER, CLAUDE,
Disconnectio,
The Mise-en-Scène,
Wert and the Life Without End.

PALLEAU-PAPIN, FRANÇOISE,
This Is Not a Tragedy: The Works of David
Markson.

PINGET, ROBERT,
The Inquisitory,
Mahu or The Material,
Trio.

QUENEAU, RAYMOND,
The Last Days ,
Odile,
Pierrot Mon Ami,
Saint Glinglin.

RICARDOU, JEAN,
Place Names.

FOR A FULL LIST OF PUBLICATIONS, VISIT: www.dalkeyarchive.com

ROBBE-GRILLET,
Project for a Revolution in New York.

ROCHE, MAURICE,
Compact.

ROHE, OLIVER,
Origin Unknown.

ROLIN, JEAN,
The Explosion of the Radiator Hose.

ROLIN, OLIVIER,
Hotel Crystal.

ROUBAUD, ALIX CLEO,
Alix's Journal.

ROUBAUD, JACQUES,
The Form of a City Changes Faster,
Alas,
Than the Human Heart,
The Great Fire of London,
Hortense in Exile,
Hortense Is Abducted,
The Loop,
Mathematics,
The Plurality of Worlds of Lewis,
The Princess Hoppy or, The Tale of Labrador,
Some Thing Black.

ROUSSEL, RAYMOND,
Impressions of Africa.

SALVAYRE, LYDIE,
The Company of Ghosts,
Everyday Life,
The Lecture,
Portrait of the Writer as a Domesticated Animal,
The Power of Flies.

SARRAUTE, NATHALIE,
Do You Hear Them?,
Martereau,
The Planetarium.

SIMON, CLAUDE,
The Invitation.

SINIAC, PIERRE,
The Collaborators.

VIAN, BORIS,
Heartsnatcher.

VIRCONDELET, ALAIN,
Duras: A Biography.